OHIO
DOMINICAN
UNIVERSITY™

SINCE 1911

ESCAPING TORNADO SEASON

a story in poems

ESCAPING TORNADO SEASON

JULIE WILLIAMS

HarperTempest
An Imprint of HarperCollins*Publishers*

Escaping Tornado Season
Copyright © 2004 by Julie Williams

Library of Congress Cataloging-in-Publication Data
Escaping tornado season : a story in poems / Julie Williams.—1st ed.
    p.   cm.
    Summary: Poems describe how thirteen-year-old Allie, living with
her grandparents in a small Minnesota town in the 1960s, struggles
to cope with her father's recent death, being abandoned by her
mother, and trying to fit in at school.
    ISBN 0-06-008639-4 — ISBN 0-06-008640-8 (lib. bdg.)
    1. Girls—Juvenile poetry. 2. Separation (Psychology)—Juvenile
poetry. 3. Grandparent and child—Juvenile poetry. 4. Maternal
deprivation—Juvenile poetry. 5. Abandoned children—Juvenile
poetry. 6. Fathers—Death—Juvenile poetry. 7. Minnesota—Juvenile
poetry. 8. Children's poetry, American. [1. Separation (Psycho-
logy)—Poetry. 2. Grief—Poetry. 3. Family life—Poetry. 4. Schools—
Poetry. 5. Minnesota—Poetry. 6. American Poetry.] I. Title.
PS3573.I44963E83 2004   2003009330
811'.6—dc22   CIP
                                                                 AC

Typography by Sasha Illingworth
1 2 3 4 5 6 7 8 9 10
❖
First Edition

TO GORDON & JENNIFER

NORTHERN MINNESOTA

EARLY 1960s

RUNNING FOR THE STORM CELLAR

A funnel, someone shouts, a funnel! Get the kids!

And we are rounded up from where we stand
watching wild horses gather in the sky
Run for the storm cellar
Run fast as we can

Down we go into the earth
huddle together in the
light from Daddy's
lantern, sheltered
by what's left of
last year's
carrots &
potatoes

Waiting
for the
tornado
to blow
over . . .

THERE'S NO ESCAPING
TORNADO SEASON

Last month when my dad finally came home
from the hospital, every afternoon
I read to him for an hour or so

Mostly Mom made me read from the Bible

I'd pull my chair up as close as I could get
to where he lay on the bed in my room
but before I even cracked the Bible open
he'd say, *You know, Allie, I liked that one*
you read from the other day
about that Dorothy girl
her goofy little dog, the yellow brick road
& the big twister . . .

It was right there on the night table waiting
The Wizard of Oz, Daddy! I'd say
and open up to the place we left off
the day before

One time Mom walked by
on her way to the bathroom
and when she heard what I was reading
she started in muttering, how she does
about tornadoes & hard times

Your mom's always trying to escape
tornado season, Allie . . .
Daddy said, soon as she was out of earshot
and I nodded, though I wasn't sure
what he meant

I read some more and then he said
You might as well know now, Allie
there's no escaping . . .

There's no escaping tornado season.

BUT EVERY YEAR MOM TRIES

She can stand Nebraska fall & winter
but come spring when twisters dip
from clouds, she starts to itch for
Northern Minnesota
for crystal clear water
& cool breezy nights
for Gram's chicken potpie
& Gramps painting in the garage

So every year since I can remember
we packed up & drove north
to lakes & pine trees
lit up by northern lights
to stay till Labor Day
when Daddy'd drive back up
to bring us home
to Nebraska again

Summer was his busy time
piloting a tugboat on the Missouri River
building bridges, shoring up pilings
to keep that muddy water
from eating up people's houses
from lapping at their front porches
from drowning their crops
the way it does every time it floods

But Daddy died three days ago
so today it was Daddy's brother
my Uncle Wayne
who drove us to Minnesota
our car following the hearse
with Daddy in it
all the way

& that means
from now on
it's just me

& Mom.

UNDER THE WEEPING WILLOW

The hearse turns right at the intersection
on its way to Taylor Brothers
funeral home, but
Uncle Wayne turns left
& there's Gram
under the weeping willow
our first glimpse
of the Big House on the hill
& the Little House peeking out from behind
Gram is waiting, watching for us to arrive

There they are! Her hands fly up to her face
& even though we are still too far away to see
I know tears are rolling faster
than her snatched hankie can catch them

Now we're up the drive

There's Gramps in the garage
paintbrush in one hand, he's waving with the other
He lopes out to meet our '57 Ford & in a flash
we are all arms & legs & hands & necks
wrapped around, welcoming
this muddled huddle of family

Maggie! Allie! Gram sobs, *Our girls
our girls . . .*

Uncle Wayne removes his hat
& wipes his brow. He takes
a swipe at his eyes while he's at it

Gramps stares hard at the paintbrush
he's holding
so the tears in his eyes
won't fall

I have to swallow & swallow
around the lump in my throat
before I can say one word

and I end up to be
the only one
not crying.

ON MEMORIAL DAY WE
GO TO THE CEMETERY

We go every year to tend the family graves
especially my brother Tuck's
but this year there's a service
graveside
for Daddy

A big rectangular hole, deep
rich dark smell of earth freshly dug

Gramps nods at my mother
& she goes forward
tosses her handful of dirt down

It thuds on the casket, a hard hollow sound

Gramps nods at me
my turn to step forward, toss my handful of dirt
I don't want to do it
I don't want to stand on the edge of that hole
hear that hollow thud again

But my mother is looking at me
Gramps, the minister
Gram sobbing into her hankie
looking off in another direction
toward the pines

I hear Daddy say to me
clear like he's right there beside me
That's not me down there any more
You go ahead, toss that dirt down
it'll make your mother feel better

You know your grandpa won't go on till you do.

IT'S LIKE HE'S RIGHT THERE
TALKING TO ME

A cool breeze hits the side of my face
wraps itself around my shoulder

I turn real quick, but not quick enough

Next thing I know, my toes are on the edge
I've let loose that dirt
it trickles down on the casket
without hardly making a sound

Gram & Gramps follow
and then men begin to shovel dirt in
filling up that hole

The minister prays & Mom falls to pieces
but Gramps is there to catch her

We walk back to his black Studebaker and get in
drive real slow to the Big House on the hill
where all the people wait
with pies & hot dishes & stories.

THE WOMEN TELL ME STORIES
LOUD ENOUGH FOR MOM TO HEAR

Your father never gave up grieving the son he lost, Gram says
Your twin, that little boy made him so proud
To lose him like that
It broke his spirit, she says
taking care of your mother and trying to hide his pain
Men are like that, she says, *They need a son*
Keeps them knowing they're a man

Your mother broke his spirit, Auntie Win says
She got crazy after that boy died
acted a fool, blamed him
He broke his back bending to please her
but there was no pleasing her
It was your mother's fault he died

Your mother was looking for a man like her father
Aunt Ida tells me in a conspiratorial whisper
but I'm afraid she never found him
Your grandfather, now, he's one of a kind
The good Lord broke the mold when
He made your grandfather.

I'M STILL NOT CRYING,
SO TODAY'S THE DAY

Mom's brother, my Uncle Jake
decides today's the day
to teach me how to spit
further than my cousins
He says you have to
think salivating thoughts
slick your lips so,
and blow like hell
Then he pats my behind
tells me I'm built
like a French
      brick
      shit-house
Purses up his lips
and sends a wad flying
way beyond ours

You cut that out, Auntie Win says,
Wait till I get you home, Jake
& drags me inside to give me
the most beautiful orange & gold
flowered chiffon scarf
almost big as a shawl
& sparkling in the sunlight

When my mother sees it she says
Is that any kind of a gift to give a child, Win?
Especially today . . . and tries to give it back
I fuss like a little kid so I get to keep it
Tonight I'm sleeping with it under my pillow
or I know Mom'll take it away
To keep until Allie's older.

IN THREE MONTHS
I'M TURNING FOURTEEN

In ninth grade come fall. Back home
in Nebraska, especially since
we moved into town
I've finally started
to make some friends

Four more years left of school
& even now
with my father buried here
I'd rather be in tornado country
than Northern Minnesota
any old day

The only houses close to
Gram & Gramps
are full of old people

Well, there's
Kris Svedstrom next door
but he's a junior
in high school

Gram says the Svedstroms
are like family
and I guess she's right

Kris is more like
my Nebraska cousins
way too grown
to want to spend
much time with me

Here it is
hardly even summer yet
and already I'm wishing
it was time
to go home.

ESCAPING DOWN TO THE LAKE

Slide out of tight patent leather shoes
slip out side door & run
away from relatives, away from Mom
till I'm out of sight of both houses
the Big House & the Little
run down through sumac bushes
still spring green
down rocky road to beach

I'm surprised to see Kris
perched up high on a boulder
tossing pebbles into waves
looking like he's waiting
for someone
I'm sure it's not me

Kris plays all the sports in school
but he's a star basketball player
Here, he's got a handful of pebbles
& the way he's pitching them
I can see that imaginary basket
& he's dunking every one

Nicest thing about Kris is
you don't have to talk much
around him

We sit quiet a long time
listening to the lake
lapping against rocks
sudden screeches of gulls flying
Birds chirp in trees, too
soft musical sounds
It's only the end of May
and there's still a chill in the air
my feet freezing from where
I waded in water
to climb up on this rock

*How you going to like living here
year-round?* Kris asks

A nerve jumps in my stomach
I swear it splashes down
just like a fish.

TURNING TO STONE

I don't know what Kris is talking about
us living here year-round

He reaches underwater
brings up a handful of stones
pitches them one after
another out into the lake
They land, *plunk, plunk, plunk*
Grabs up another handful, sends them
flying one at a time, out into the water

That's what your gram told my mom,
is all he says and I know

it will turn out to be so

I can't say a word, just sit there
wishing I could
click my heels together
like Dorothy in Oz
only find myself
in Nebraska not Kansas

In Nebraska
instead of here
staring at the ruffled water
as if I had turned
to stone.

I HATE MY MOTHER

Most days I keep my mouth shut
thinking maybe it'll change
Daddy could make me
half like her he loved her so

Not now

I love my grandpa but
when he & Mom get together
they are all smiles & stories, pushing
Gram & Daddy & me to the edges of
everything

Daddy & I were like
mashed potatoes & gravy
like rice & beans
like fried onions on a good burger

With Mom, I'm the mustard or
something puckers your mouth up
horseradish maybe
that thing you forget in the refrigerator
get along just fine without.

WHERE DO THE WORDS GO?

After I went back to the house
after Uncle Jake & Auntie Win went home
when all the other relatives & neighbors
were gone, too
I opened my mouth to tell Mom
how mad I am that we
have to move here
that she didn't even
tell me we were
moving here
to say all those words
that were
gathering
inside my head
hooking themselves to each other
piling up & pushing away any other thoughts

I opened my mouth to say them
and nothing came out

Where do the words go, I wonder

It must be someplace quiet
& deadly calm
like the eye of a tornado
or the center of one of those
whirlpools Daddy worked so hard
to steer his boat away from

Or maybe they fall
with liquid *plunks*
like the stones Kris tossed
into the water of the bay

Where do they go
those twirling, swirling
hot muggy tornado
words . . .

So much easier
to write down
than to
say.

DADDY ALWAYS HATED GOOD-BYES

He refused to say the word

Each time he left us for the summer
saw us moved into the Little House
behind the Big House
on the hill
drove off down
the road

He'd hug & kiss us all

He'd wave & grin
& wave again
but he refused to say good-bye

Today when Uncle Wayne
got up so early
& left to catch a Greyhound bus
heading back home
to Nebraska
I thought about
my dad &
all the good-byes he never said

And I hugged Uncle Wayne
extra hard, said
See you real soon . . .

And in the back of my mind
you know what
I'm thinking

I hate to say good-bye.

CALLING GRAMPS

It's Saturday again
I wake up early
smell potatoes Gram's frying
down in the basement kitchen
take stairs from the attic
two at a time
jump off the landing
at the bottom

Allie, go call your grandfather to breakfast
Gram yells soon as
she hears me and
I run to do
what she says

Scent of sun filtered through dust
oil paint & turpentine
wood shavings, cedar, pine

Feel of canvas stretched tight
to wooden frame, sawdust
grit sticks to fingers, under nails
pine stool rubbed smooth
by paint-spattered pants

Sound of brush pushing paint
sweeping an expanse
splotting small shapes
bees humming outside
in morning glory vine, occasional
drone of mosquito

Sight of colors growing a forest
lake rippling stream
a deer licking salt & by her side
a wobbly-legged freckled fawn . . .

Gramps in the garage on a brisk
barely summer day, wielding bristled brush

Paint, the color of remembering.

AND DIDN'T EVEN SAY GOOD-BYE

Up the driveway, halfway back to the house
from Gramps's garage
I see our car's
not there

She's gone, isn't she? I ask Gramps
but I already know the answer

Mom's done it again
She's gone and she didn't even
say good-bye

She'll be back, Allie, Gramps says
Of course she'll be back

Gram turns away from the stove
looks me straight in the eye
*Do you really think
she's going to stay down there
in Nebraska with all those relatives
of your dad's
she hates so much?*

Now someone's actually
making sense
and for some reason
it cheers me up enough
so I make it through the day.

MAKING IT THROUGH THE DAY

And it's a day of mingled rain & sun
dandelions popping up everywhere
spreading a carpet of yellow over the hill

Gram hands me her big iron pot
with wooden handles

Now, Allie, you go gather me up
the tenderest leaves & buds
that haven't opened yet, she says
& I'll cook you up a mess of greens
for supper

For Gram's greens & gravy
I'd gather a mountain of dandelions

You got to get them before they get too
stringy or before your grandpa
mows 'em down . . .

Gramps went to Pete Patruski's store
for cream to color Gram's coffee
He was gone a long time
and carried home
a jar of pickled pigs' feet
a package of Fig Newtons
a dozen powdered sugar doughnuts

and forgot the cream

I borrowed some from
old Mrs. Paulson next door
when I took her the mail

Gram's got the coffee on

Looks like tonight we'll have a feast.

THIS IS LIKE MY MOTHER

This is like my mother
taking off in the middle of the night
without telling me good-bye

This is like my mother

How she does things

Like three years ago in Nebraska
when we lived out at the river
in our house on stilts
right next to Uncle Wayne & Aunt Lulu
on our little farm Daddy & I loved

One day I walked home from school
and the house stood empty, cleaned out
For a second I thought
Oh my gosh, they've gone & left me

The door was open & I went in
A few odds & ends in my parents' bedroom
Same in mine. An old teddy bear
leaning in a corner
A shoe I grew out of the year before
just one, not the pair

Then I heard the truck
and Daddy roared up so fast
he almost hit the porch
Jumped out & was up eight steps in two
I heard him calling out, *Sweet Pea* . . .

He grabbed me & threw me
way up in the air before he
hugged me hard
I was in sixth grade then
too big for him to do that
but he did it anyway

Where'd we move? I asked

See, Mom'd been at Daddy ever since
we got to Nebraska to get us off
the river bottom and into town
She'd really been at him
since the tornado
But I didn't recall either of them
saying we got a place

I wanted to ask why he didn't tell me
we were moving, but I bit my lip
I didn't want to hurt him or
make him feel he'd done
something wrong

I left that up to my mother.

HOW SHE DOES THINGS

Dang that woman! Daddy said then, laughing
She packed while I was on the river
& you were in school
Mudroom off the kitchen?
That thing was plumb full of boxes ready to go
Wayne   Ray   Bill
even your cousins Carl & Tommy
all lined up here to help. Allie, honey
she had everything over there by noon
Had some trouble getting the icebox
up the bend in those stairs, though,
that's why I was late . . .

So here she goes again
not telling me
we were moving to
Minnesota
not telling me
she was planning
to drop me off & run

Not telling me she'd
disappear in the middle
of the night the way she did
seven years ago
right after my twin brother, Tuck, died

She was gone a long time then

This is like my mother
How she does things.

SPRING TURNED
ITS LEAF TO SUMMER

Nobody's heard from Mom yet

She's not coming back, I say to Gram
who says, *Sure she is, she's just making
arrangements*

Oh right, I say, remembering when Mom
moved us out of the river house and into town
that time, how it took only one day

Dump another spoonful of brown sugar
on the oatmeal
Gramps makes me eat
every morning

He raises an eyebrow but
doesn't say a word
I do not like oatmeal but Gramps says
*You can't survive a Minnesota winter without it
might as well start now*
Probably I can't survive with it
but what's the point arguing something
stupid as that.

AFTER SUPPER GRAMPS
MAKES ROOT BEER FLOATS

We sit out on the hill sipping
rock back & forth in
creaky metal lawn chairs
watch cars go by on the highway

Loons fly over, calling to each other
on their way to the lake
I know they're loons because
my mother knows how to imitate their call
and Daddy used to make her
do it all the time she does it so well

Stare hard at bats diving down
from attic eaves
so Gramps won't see
I'm remembering other summers
so Gram won't know I'm remembering
anything at all.

I'M REMEMBERING HOW

Every visit Gram tells me, *There's a ghost*
in the pantry, back beneath
the stairs, between dirt-floored
root cellar & laundry room

Gram always says this while lifting stove lids
& shoving down last pieces of
splintery firewood into her
big black-bellied cookstove

That ghost is filmy cold & gray
Wraps itself around your neck
like some huge sticky spiderweb
Particularly likes little girls, she says
peering over her round-edged glasses
at me

Why, look here, she says, rising up
empty-handed from the wood bucket
I'm clean outta firewood. Run
fetch me some, quick
from that pile
back there
in the root cellar . . .

I'm remembering how Gram taught me
to play solitaire when I was seven

Gram cheated at cards
only nobody told me that
until much later when I was
demonstrating solitaire for my dad

He hit the ceiling, lit into me
told me he'd kill me

if I turned out like her . . .

I'm remembering how Mom
always used to say that Gram
kept toads & frogs for pets
when she was a little girl
Dressed them up in dolls' clothes
and let the dolls lie naked
under the attic eaves

Then she'd push her dressed-up
friends around all day
in her doll buggy

Scared the bejesus out of
old Mrs. Paulson next door

Mom said Gram liked reptiles
better than she liked people

She still does.

MAKING IT THROUGH THE NIGHT

The bats loop & arc
graceful as swallows dark
against a darkening sky
Gram says they carry rabies
get stuck in your hair
Tonight I think they are dancing
or playing some game only bats know

I sip the last of my root beer
wish I could be up there flying with them

Across the bay first northern lights
of the summer flicker & dance
colored heat lightning
electric memories shimmering
over the blackboard of the night sky

Our lawn chairs creak back & forth
louder than the frogs
in the deep marsh
across the road
I can feel Gram's eyes
boring into the side of my head
but I don't turn around

I'm too busy remembering how
in happy syncopation with
Mom's loon sounds
Daddy would be making
frog sounds, too.

IT'S TOURIST SEASON NOW

All day long & up till dark
tourists park their cars out on the road
walk up the long, hilly drive to see
up close the painting Gramps did
on the inside of the garage door

Then they look at Gramps's canvases
& I try to guess whether or not
they'll buy & if they do
which one & for
how much

Today a lady asked, *May I use
the facilities?*
and when I pointed her
to our vine-covered outhouse
she gasped & said, *Oh my, how quaint!*
And I guess she forgot
she had to go

Because instead of using it
she wandered over to where
Gram sits in her lawn chair
& waits for someone
to *Come & sit a spell . . .*

When they do
oh my
the stories
Gram can tell.

GRAM SITS A SPELL

Don't tell our whole life story
to strangers, my mom'd always say
to Gram, who told it all
to anyone she met
anywhere
if you left her alone
for two minutes

We'd find her sitting somewhere
wiping tears from her eyes, words like

That precious angel, thank God
we could give him a decent burial

still hanging, hot & humid
in the cool evening air.

A GREEN INK LETTER

A letter came today from my mother
one of her green ink letters
like she wrote after my brother, Tuck, died
I don't know where she went then
only that she sent us letters
green ink on gray paper
with wet marks I heard
Gram say were tears

That was the other time I came to stay
with Gram & Gramps
went to third grade
in the school
up top of the hill
He didn't have to, but
every day Gramps walked
to meet me halfway

If there was a letter with green words
after supper Gram put her glasses on
read it out loud
Dear folks, she'd start, then a quick
glance at me, *& my dearest Allie* . . .

I found the letters a while ago
tucked away under Gram's fancywork
in a bureau drawer
The truth is they weren't to me at all
Every single one begins plain
Dear Folks

MORE GREEN INK WORDS

There are no tears staining this letter
only green ink words telling Gramps
she'll stay down in Nebraska till
she gets things settled
not to worry, everything's fine
there's just a lot to do

She's packing up all our dishes & books
& cookware & pictures & winter clothes
& everything else she can get in crates
& boxes, but she's selling the furniture

Daddy's clothes she's parceling out
to all his brothers
Uncle Wayne will buy the farm
and Mom gave him Daddy's boat

In fact, she says, all the aunts & uncles
Daddy's brothers & sisters
send their love and wonder
what Gramps is painting this season
whether Gram is still baking those
delicious blueberry pies
They miss me, too, Mom says
wonder how their Sweet Pea is doing

She'll be back, she says
as soon as she gets things tied up
down there.

AIRING IT OUT

*You've got to let your mom deal with this
in her own way*, Gram says
We've pulled a kitchen chair
out on the lawn under
twin birch trees
Gramps planted when
Tuck & I were born
I'm brushing Gram's hair

When you undo her braids
her hair reaches all the way
to the ground
She likes me to brush it hard
& scratch her scalp with a comb
Then she pulls her chair
out into the soft sunshine
while a breeze picks up
her hair and blows it
this way & that

Airing it out, she calls it
Between washings

When it's aired, I brush
the tangles out again
& braid it back
into two tight braids
hand her hairpins
and she winds it
round & round
her head, pinning it
with deft strokes
back into its
brown & gray crown

Yeah, I think, holding back
from airing out my words

But what about me?

DEPRESSION PUDDING

Why don't you write your mother a letter?

Gram's pouring milk over bits of bread
I've torn into my cup

You're such a good letter writer . . .

I watch her while she adds sugar &
colors it all with a little coffee
dark from the pot
pushed back on the woodstove

She'd like a letter from you, Gram says

I duck my head down and slurp
the mess of bread & milk & coffee & sugar
Gramps calls Depression Pudding

I don't tell Gram about the letters
I've already written Mom
or how afraid I am
Mom's not writing because
she's never coming back again

Instead I tear another piece of bread
into my cup and hold it out
for Gram to pour
milk & sugar & coffee . . .

I like that name: Depression Pudding.

I SHOULD BE USED TO BEING
BY MYSELF, BUT I'M NOT

When Tuck was alive
he & I were always together
we even slept in
the same room
That way Mom knew
I would hear him
in the night
if he awoke scared
or sick or needing her
and I could run to get her
to let her know

When I went to school
for the little time
Tuck was well enough
to go, I became
his eyes & ears & arms & legs
& coursing blood
the one who could run & play
and then return to tell him all about it

Back then I never
had any friends
because
no one could come to the house
for fear they'd spread germs
or get him too excited
so he & I did everything
together
but mostly I did things
for him
and raced back afterwards
to tell him all about it

His way of pretending was
to paint pictures & draw

My way was to find the words.

FINDING THE GRANDMA WORDS

Kris Svedstrom's grandma
is here from the Cities
to visit

This is the first time I've met
Grandma Svedstrom
She's skinny as a fence post
way shorter than me
she's only about four feet tall

I can't believe she's a grandma

Grandmas are fat
If they're thin there's
something wrong with them

They're fat & peculiar & funny
They fart when they walk
They like spiders & frogs
and scaring little kids
They eat bread & onion sandwiches
for breakfast
and smell like talcum powder
At least, my grandma does.

FINALLY SOMETHING TO DO

Today Gram & I went with Gramps
to the museum
so he could touch up his stuffed ducks

The museum belongs to the village
but to me it belongs to Gramps
because he's the one who did it all
the animals & paintings & displays

Gram sits on a lawn chair by the front door
where she collects the entrance fees
while Gramps cleans & paints
working one-by-one through
each glass-case scene

Gram smiles at people as they come & go
If they stop to talk she tells them all about
my twin brother, Daddy's death
Mom's trip to Nebraska, who I am
& why I'm here

My mother would be deader than Daddy
if she knew.

THIS SUMMER DRUMMING

We stay for the powwow on the museum lawn
It's Gramps's job to collect the money
from the tourists and pay the dancers
I love to watch the Ojibwe come in from
the reservation, cars full of family
loaded down with grandmas, kids & dogs
They park in the shade, fling wide
their doors and don regalia
strung with beads & bright stitches
moccasins & headdresses
beaded purses hung over arms
shawls slung over shoulders

Once drummers begin, people gather
Old women start the circle, their up
down step in time with the beat

Young girls join them, then the men
Double-time steps in swirling circles
make me dizzy
old men chant singsong words I can't
understand but seem to recognize
Anishinaabemowin, Gramps says
ancient Ojibwe language . . .

Older'n us even, Gram says with a laugh

I follow close behind Gramps
as he gives the dancers their pay
then we hoist Gram into the Studebaker
ride the Black Beetle home
drums still playing
behind us
in late summer dark.

GIFT OF A KITTEN

Today when I stopped at Patruski's General Store
Mrs. Patruski took me out back
and she hollered to the boy
who works there
Joey Redfern! she shouted
I've noticed before
she always says his full name
Joey Redfern, give this girl one of those kittens

And out of the woodpile
he lifted a tiny golden fluff of a kitten
held her up against
his dark face & shock of black hair
before he handed her
oh so gentle to me

I named her Kitsy and
Gramps made a box for her
down in the kitchen
behind Gram's woodstove

At night, though, she creeps through
living room & up curving stairs
to the attic where
she curls around my ankles
stays purring until daybreak
when I open my window
& let her out on the roof
that slopes down
so close to the ground
she can jump

So can I.

WHEN GRAM REMEMBERS
MY BROTHER

Tears spring to the corners of her eyes
out comes hankie, one I spent
Saturday pressing with irons kept hot
on her cast-iron cookstove
pressing tiny violets flat as memories

Today she remembered how much
Tuck liked to color at the kitchen table
while she cooked
While you ran in & out, she says
bringing him things
Letting flies & mosquitoes
in with me
every screen door slam

She stuffs her wrinkled hankie
see how the violets spring
to three-dimensional form
into the waistband of her dress
glares at me with all her soft
wetness turned to sudden ice

Don't you even miss your
brother? she spits

And here I go again

Making the screen door
slam
behind me.

IT TURNS OUT KITSY IS A BOY

A regular tomcat, Gram says
shooing Kitsy out of the kitchen
but only after she's given him
pieces of leftover walleye
from last night's supper

What're you going to call him now?
Gramps asks. I don't know
He comes when I call him Kitsy
Seems to me a cat has more
sense than to care about
a little thing like that.

WAITING FOR THE APPLES

Today I stole crab apples
from Johnsons' orchard
gathered good ones
from the ground
crammed my sweatshirt pouch full
& nearly peed my pants
for fear Mrs. Johnson would come
yelling & waving
her dish towel
the way she did last time

I had to crawl across the gully
and run down the railroad tracks
before I could cut through woods
to the springs

Then I put the sun-warm crab apples
to soak in icy water and sat there

wishing school wasn't starting
next week, wishing my dad
was still alive
pretending Tuck was here
with me so
if I have to go
to school here
at least we could
go together

trying not to think
about my mother

I sat there for a long time
like that, telling myself
lies that pass
for stories

waiting for the apples
to crunch cold.

IT'S MY BIRTHDAY

Today I turned fourteen

Uncle Jake & Auntie Win came down from Bemidji
Great-great-aunt Ida came over
from her little cottage
on the other side of the swamp
Mr. & Mrs. Svedstrom came over, too

Kris had football practice & couldn't come

Gram made baking powder biscuits, fried chicken
mashed potatoes & gravy, added bacon to
green beans Mom canned last summer

Auntie Win baked an angel food cake with pink frosting

I got a new sweater, pair of penny loafers
and a bunch of socks & underwear, probably because
school is starting tomorrow and
none of last year's fit me anymore
Gramps says I've shot up like a weed

Uncle Wayne & Aunt Lulu sent a card
& a five-dollar bill
said get some school supplies with it
and I will

Mom didn't send anything or call
at the Svedstroms' or even write

But then every year
since my twin brother died
it was Daddy who bought presents
& made sure we celebrated my birthday

so this year I really didn't
expect anything at all.

IT'S THE FIRST DAY OF SCHOOL
& IT'S RAINING

Gram made me
put on my old jacket because
she's still waiting for Mom to get here
and buy me a new one

Spring before last my dad got me
this black corduroy jacket and
when I put it on I felt beautiful
It was a toss-your-shoulders-back
I'm-on-top-of-the-world piece of clothing
I wore it every day until my mother threatened
to throw it away unless I gave it a rest

Now the arms are too short
& the shoulders pinch
When I get home from school
I'm folding it up, sticking it in a box
in a cupboard under the eaves

I don't care if it rains buckets
I don't care if it snows
I'm not wearing it again.

HIDING MY FACE

Gramps asked if I wanted
a ride to school but I said, *No I'll walk*

When I got to Patruski's General Store
two girls Gram told me are in my grade
came out talking & laughing

I smiled at them, but they were so busy
they didn't even see, so
I slowed down and let them walk ahead

All the way up the hill to school
their laughter floated back to me
on the chilly wind. And I was glad
the cold rain hid the redness of my face
behind its September storm.

HIDING IN THE BATHROOM

I hate school. Everyone stares at me
wearing last year's clothes
& the same sweater every day
There's a dress code here
& my skirts are too short
I have to hide from Mr. Walter, the principal
He makes girls kneel to show their hems
if they touch the wood floor
I know mine won't
and not because they're in style

All homeroom today I hid in the bathroom
heard those girls from
the first day
their names are Ardis & Christine
laughing while they combed their hair
talking about tourists & summer girls
how stupid we all are

They left finally and I managed
to sneak past Mr. Walter when he was
yelling at one of the Onigum kids

I hate school
And even though I still
hate my mom
I wish she would come home.

THAT BLACK-HAIRED CAT BOY

It turns out Joey Redfern is in
all my classes at school
I wonder why Gram never
mentioned that when she was
pointing out all those
other kids, maybe because
he's a boy

It seems like he's forgotten
about that day back by
Pete Patruski's woodpile
when he picked out
Kitsy for me

or all the times
we've smiled & said hi
when I've stopped
at the store to pick up
Gram's milk & bread & cream

I found out today
at the pep rally that
he's on the junior varsity
football team.

YESTERDAY WE HAD
TO WRITE A COMPOSITION

What we did on our summer vacation

I didn't mean to, but I wrote about
Daddy dying and
what it was like
bringing him up here
to bury him
and then I had to turn it in

Today right at the end of class
Mr. Borden made me read it out loud
and all I could hear was kids snickering
& shuffling papers & whispering
behind their hands

Two boys in the back row were laughing
and Mr. Borden didn't even stop them
just made me keep reading
until it was done

I tore it up
and dropped it in the water
off the city dock on my way home

Watched that big red *A* float for a few feet
then get pulled under a whitecap
& drown.

LIDIA WHITE CLOUD READS ALOUD

Today Mr. Borden chose other kids to read
summer compositions: boating trips & fishing
family vacations, carnivals, fireworks
Fourth of July parades

I put my head down while one girl read
about training a new puppy, another
the horse she took to the county fair

My mother sickened & died this summer
a new voice said and I had to hold myself still
so I wouldn't jerk my head up to see who
was reading words out loud in this way

I helped my grandmother prepare my mother
for her grave. We practice Midewiwin, the Old Ways
We put her in the ground & I helped my father
build a grave house to put above her

The room fills with jeers & snickers
but the voice grows stronger

Before she died, my mother gave me
a beaded dress to remember her by
When she was gone, my father & I
gathered many small things she had loved
& put them in the grave house
so that she would never feel alone

This month when we go after manoomin
we will dedicate the wild rice we gather
to the memory of my mother
Next year we will visit her grave house again
leave food & memories for her spirit
There will never be a time when I will stop missing her

When I look up, dark gray eyes
clear & clean as an autumn wave
hold my gaze, a mouth set in firm lines
flickers for a moment toward a smile.

A RUSH OF REMEMBERING

Lidia White Cloud's words
brought back those spring days
down in Nebraska
hot as the underbelly of
one of Uncle Wayne's hogs

Out there on the Missouri River
a breeze might riffle hair
dry for a second at least
damp sheen of sweat sitting on skin

Inside our place, in town
second floor up
big old house Mom rented
across the street from
city park & municipal pool
it was more than hot

It was an oven baking
cookies all day

A holiday house with
no good smells

Tornado weather, Uncle Wayne said
each time he stopped by
Aunts & uncles brought fans
We stuck one in every room
and two in Daddy's
All they did was move hot
wet air around, make it worse
but we kept them going anyway

Something about their hum
& whish of air felt like hope
like he would get better when I knew
from feet bottoms to the deep
inside pounding of my heart
he wouldn't.

THERE WILL NEVER BE A TIME
WHEN I WILL STOP MISSING HIM

Daddy took a drink of water
I wiped his forehead with a cool cloth
He'd been sick in bed all spring
Lung cancer, I heard the doctor tell Mom
so far gone when they
operated on him in March
they sewed him back up
gave him radiation treatments

He had a big scar
where they cut into him
& weird markings on his back

Doc Gerring said he got the cancer
from smoking so many cigarettes all these years
I don't know
Makes sense, I suppose, but
Grandpa Benton always used to say
smoking made you healthy
kept cold germs away

He died of cancer, too.

One night I was sitting up with Daddy
I asked him what made my mother hate the river so

Maggie just don't like the way
they call us river rats
he said with a dry cough

I could hear my mother muttering
This godforsaken place
What your father sees in this hellhole
of sand & snakes & sandburs is beyond me

She's afraid the river'll cut a new channel
one of these days, Daddy said
and then imitating Mom
This house'll be floating down the river
like that tugboat of yours

An accidental houseboat, I said
and my dad laughed right out loud.

I was with Daddy the night he died
He sat up suddenly on the side of the bed
said he was feeling better
I think I can sleep real well tonight, he said
Called me Sweet Pea, the way he did sometimes
I plumped his pillow, smoothed his hair
and then I lay down on my cot
And I fell asleep, too
Hard, not like usual times
I was watching him

Right before dawn something woke me
Felt like a cool breeze coming from Daddy's bed
Oh my gosh, I thought, a storm's come up
got to shut the window
But when I looked, nothing moved the curtains
and air was hot & still

As light gathered, shadows disappeared
all of a sudden I thought

Maybe Daddy's a little too peaceful.

My father lay in death, curled up on his side
Hands tucked under his chin
A smile lingered around his mouth
pain lines miraculously removed

Cancer smell singeing nostrils
rotting flesh still ripe in the room
as usual I tried to keep my mouth closed
so the smell wouldn't touch my tongue

His skin was cool, though, & soft
My kiss on his cheek smacked hollow

He was gone.

My mother turned the mattress
after my father died
and gave me back my room
She left the bathroom light on
and my door open a crack
for it to show through

I don't need it

My father's presence
lights the room.

Seeing Uncle Wayne cry buckets at the service
back home in Nebraska
got me going till somehow
I couldn't stop
Mom starting in to shake me
hissing at me hard

Best let her cry, Aunt Bentie said
but Mom turned away
She hates Aunt Bentie like poison

Come to think of it
she's not crazy about any of Daddy's
brothers & sisters

Don't do like your Aunt Bentie, my father said
on his almost last breath
My baby sister, she's a drunk & a whore
Red hair's straight out of a bottle
Funny she doesn't drink the damn stuff

Don't end up a drunk, he said, bony claws
of his once huge hand circling my wrist

Only thing worse than a whore
is a drunken woman.

IT'S WILD RICING TIME

School just started and already
this week all the kids from Onigum
are missing
When they're here
they keep to themselves
but with them gone
halls seem empty, ghosted
Classrooms echo
Mr. Lindstrom's paddle gathers dust
on the corner of his desk
Mr. Borden's fingers twitch
you know they itch to grab
& shake someone who isn't there
Teachers are left with no one to knock around
except some greaser boys from Hackensack
who ride their motorcycles to school
so day after day they're catching hell.

AT SUPPER TIME WE HEAR
THE DRUMS

Their beat carries
across the waters of the bay

Over there in a place I've never been
I imagine
Lidia & her father gathering wild rice together
celebrating the life & death
of Lidia's mother

I ask Gramps about it and he tells me
how they knock rice into a flat-bottom boat
with sticks, how old women & children wait
in camp for the ricers to return, prepare a feast
How as night draws itself up & gathers
around them, old men begin to beat
the ceremonial drum

In my mind, Lidia's words
are drumbeats
Lidia's story
washes over me
like a healing rain
And I hope she will be
among the kids who return
to school again
when the wild ricing is over.

EACH DAY THE AIR
IS A LITTLE COLDER

Blue in the lake is a little deeper
Blue in the sky a little brighter
Yellow, gold, orange & red leaves on trees
color a little sharper

I rush to the post office on my way home
from school each day
but since that first green ink letter
no word comes from my mother

After the post office I stop at the store
there's no football practice on Fridays
so Joey Redfern is there
to wrap up Gram's ears of corn
& show me the best apples
from Mrs. Patruski's orchard

At home, the brisk wind makes Kitsy's ears lie flat
& he pounces like a wild beast
into piles of leaves I rake up after school

At night we hear the drumming
across the bay in Onigum and
I wonder what Lidia is doing
how much wild rice her father
harvested today.

SOME CHOICES

I ask Joey Redfern
how come he isn't out of school
and he says

They'd disqualify me
from football . . .

and I don't know
what to say
so I don't say
anything
and he adds

Besides, no one in my family
down here
goes ricing

I ask him, *What do you mean*
down here? and he says

We're the only ones
live down here on Leech
My cousins up at Red Lake
they all go ricing

He pauses for a second
then he says
& they still get to play football
when the ricing's done.

ON THIS SIDE OF THE BAY TODAY

Gramps & I took down summer screens
put up storm windows
in both houses
the Big House & the Little

Storm windows on frames
with heavy plastic stretched tight over them
that blur the glass

You can't see out . . .
You can't see in . . .

Light comes through like in a painting
we studied in art class last year
soft & holy

The house feels smaller, brittle
like cold might reach through
& crack us all into little pieces.

AT HOME WE STACK FIREWOOD

Today Gramps borrowed the truck
from Patruski's General Store
and we drove way out in the woods past Onigum
to the mill for firewood, enough to last
all the way through winter

There's already a big stack from trees
off our back acre, but now we need a lot more
Gramps says, *To keep the wood furnace burning*
in the Little House once Mom comes

If Mom comes, I think

And to heat
the cookstove at their place
for all those big Sunday dinners
he & Gram plan to have

What big Sunday dinners? I ask

For the four of us, he says
And the six of us when Jake & Win come
the seven of us with Aunt Ida
And there's always the Svedstroms
Gramps adds, *that makes it ten*
Who knows? We might even have Mrs. Paulson

I try to picture dinner for a dozen
'cause I'm counting Kitsy
in Gram's tiny basement kitchen
her so fat pulling roast chickens
from that old woodstove
almost bust a gut laughing

Gramps laughs with me

We unload three cords of firewood & stack two
wood house nearly filled to bursting
root cellar stack piled high
us so tired we can hardly eat a chicken potpie
Gram made us while we were gone.

WHAT I KEEP WONDERING

In the morning, I could swear
the blue in the lake is deeper still
blue sky up a notch brighter

Autumn leaves on trees, once vivid as water & sky
begin to grow dull & fall to the ground

I see loons and ducks flying away
heading south, but no word
comes from my mother

Every night now we hear the drums
moving across the bay
from Onigum

How come the drums sound so close?
I ask & Gramps answers,
They walk across the water
just as Gram says
It's only three miles across the bay

I wonder if Lidia goes with her father
& helps him harvest the rice
If when they come home at night
she helps the women
cook the supper

and when the meal
is over, I wonder if
she is with the children dancing

and through it all
what I keep wondering
is how Lidia did that to me
with her words.

BRINGING THE OUTHOUSE INDOORS

Over in the Little House
Gramps & I put in a toilet, build walls
around it with particle board

Don't suppose your mom will use the outhouse, he says

I don't blame her, I think, but hold my tongue

It's cold enough outside now
Gram & I share a chamber pot
she keeps in her bedroom
I nearly freeze creeping down the attic stairs
each time I need to pee
Gramps uses a coffee can in his room
above the kitchen
& Kitsy hurries to use his litter box
back in the cold hall on the way
to the root cellar

In the Little House basement it's freezing already
& even though the furnace is right there
on the other side of our new wall
I don't see how Mom & I
can use this toilet either
it's like bringing the outhouse indoors

I remember our nice warm bathroom
in our second floor apartment
back in Nebraska
My teeth chatter at the thought
of how frigid this seat will be
once snow sets in.

LETTING THE LITTLE HOUSE
BUILD UP HEAT

Today Gramps & I fired up the Little House furnace
loaded it with pine & birch, built a roaring blaze
Heat shot up through square metal floor vent
warming kitchen, spreading throughout
the three tiny rooms

Gramps says we're making it ready
for when Mom gets here
but I've stopped believing she's coming
and they won't make me stay over here by myself

So, what's the point?

We had to stay a long time tending the fire &
letting the house fill up with heat

Gramps went & got the Chinese checker board
a box of marbles

Gram brought a big pot of soup

I brought Kitsy

After we ate, we sat & played checkers
waiting for the fire to die down

When it was finally out
& we were shivering
we went back home
to bed.

IN THE HALL TODAY

Lidia & the other Ojibwe kids are back
most of them anyway
You'd think they're Ping-Pong balls
the way they ricochet off lockers
Mr. Walter had a whole row of kids
lined up on their knees in the gym
caught making loud whooping sounds
running in the halls

War whoops! Lidia whispers to me
with a sudden smile as she
passes my open locker
but she's gone before
I can say a word in reply.

THE LAST PREPARATION
BEFORE WINTER

When I got home from school today
Gramps had moved his garage studio
into the house and tonight
he is painting a picture
of a sunset lake & some loons
Smell of turpentine & oils mingles
with Gram's cooking wafting up
basement stairs
Paint smells, wood smoke & coffee
tickle my nose & tingle the back of my tongue

What's for dinner, Ma? Gramps shouts
hand poised to brush umber.

ANOTHER FRIDAY WITHOUT JEANS

Friday is jeans day at school and I don't have any
at least not any that fit
I try to tell Gram & Gramps that
but both of them look at me
like I'm speaking a language they've never heard
shake their heads & say
Just because it's jeans day doesn't mean
you've got to wear jeans

I am the only one at school today
not wearing jeans
except that weird girl from
the Church of the Anointed
who wears skirts all the way
down to her ankles & old lady shoes

Some of the kids from Onigum
are wearing brand-new jeans
I wonder if that means
the wild rice harvest made extra money
Lidia's are pressed with sharp creases
& new black boots peek out from beneath

Next to her my too-short skirt & scuffed shoes
make me feel like I'm from
the Church of the Appointed Loon
so when the final bell rings I hurry to
my locker, glad the week is over

In the bottom of my locker
hidden in a paper bag is a cloth sack
It's heavy with wild rice & on the side
is stamped in red ink
White Cloud Manoomin
Leech Lake Reservation

When I look around, I see
the Onigum kids are heading out the door
on their way to the buses
Lidia's dark head turns for a second
just as she enters the open doorway

All I've got time for is a wave
and then she's gone.

ON SUNDAYS, GRAMPS
& I READ THE FUNNIES

We sit on the sofa & take turns
He likes Dick Tracy best but I like
Nancy & Sluggo, the way
Gramps's voice changes for
Dagwood & Blondie
One time he read Dondi so sad
it almost made me cry

Gramps smells like Old Spice
and when he wraps me in
under his arm, cheek against
his rough wool shirt
leaning into the radio
we listen to Paul Harvey
or the World News
while Gram rocks
& reads her Bible

Gramps argues with Paul
and I slide into
static sleep
horsehair sofa rough
as the radio reception
and Gramps's plaid shirt.

WHITE SHOULDERS
PERFUME & WORDS

Aaniin, niijikwe, Lidia whispers in my ear
as I stand by my locker, whispers
loud enough for me to hear
but not the other Ojibwe girls
who sweep by us in a wave
of dark hair & leather jackets
leaving behind a heady mix
of cigarette smoke &
White Shoulders perfume

I smile, trying to hide
my confusion

Hello, my friend, she says
this time in English

Oh! I say, can't stop the grin
oh, say it again . . .

Aaniin, niijikwe, she says
as she slams her locker door
so hard the sound echoes
like it's bouncing off
the corridor walls

Aaniin, niijikwe, I repeat
clicking my locker closed
a last small echo
in the now-empty hall.

NO MATTER HOW MANY BLANKETS

It's so cold in the attic now
I can't sleep
no matter how many blankets
Gram piles on top of me
Even with the chimney
right at the head of my bed
it doesn't warm me up

When I wake
in gray light of early morning
my breath makes frosty puffs
& my nose is icy cold
Drag bedclothes down
curving attic stairs
curl up with Kitsy on the sofa
but it's cold there too
basement fire burned down low

Better come in with me
Gram says, *but not that cat . . .*
and I see her glance toward
the Little House, like she's seeing
my mother standing there
door wide open
light falling out
making a circle in the darkness
beckoning me home.

THE FIRST BIG BLIZZARD

Snow started falling in the night
and by morning there's a foot of it
soft & fine, blowing sideways
It's the last day before Thanksgiving anyway
so they send us home at noon
the hill so slippery we slide all the way down
and kids forget to be snooty
slipping & falling & laughing
all the way to the bottom

Gram has a big pot of wild rice soup
on the stove, bread fresh out of the oven
staying warm, and she's just putting a crust
in crisscrosses over the top of an apple pie
Gramps's next favorite after blueberry

Gramps brings in a smoked whitefish
We eat it with our fingers in big chunks
and pieces of new bread, washed down
by coffee tan with cream

Dark tucks in around the house
wrapping us up like a present
and Gramps says, between sips & slurps
Sure hate to be out on the roads on a night like this
Hope all those Thanksgiving travelers are
already safe at their destinations

Outside the north wind kicks up a fuss
howls through slats in wood-house walls
rattles the back door like someone trying to come in
Gram shivers & pours us each another cup of coffee
adds cream

Closed in as we are we don't see a car
turn into the drive, don't hear car door slam
But we hear the back door open, hear boots
stamping off snow, my mother's voice
come tumbling down basement stairs

Anybody here? Mom . . . Dad . . .
It's a blizzard out there, I thought for sure
I was never going to make it home.

FOR AN HOUR OR SO

My mother grabs me & hugs me
& holds onto me like she's never
going to let me go
Look at you, she says over and over
Look at how you've grown
Oh, Allie, she says, squeezing my face
between her hands, *I missed you*

Then why did you stay away so long &
Why didn't you write me a letter?
Why didn't you call up to the Svedstroms
have Kris run down & get me so we could talk?
Why didn't you send me a birthday card?
New clothes for school?

All those questions are loud in my head
but they only make it to the back of my tongue

I sit with my mother's arm around me
while she eats a piece of pie
& drinks a cup of coffee
I sit with my mother's arm around me
while she tells the story
of her fourteen-hour drive in blinding snow
pulling that trailer
filled with all we own in this world

And as I sit with my mother's arm around me
the questions in my head seem to
fade away

and for an hour or so all I am is glad
she is finally home.

HUNKERING DOWN

When the tornado came we huddled, deep in the earth
against the dirt wall, the one in the direction we knew
for certain that funnel was coming from
Tuck wrapped up in a musty blanket
Mom had stored down there
for just such an emergency
all of us shivering in the chill

Daddy gave me his T-shirt, sat there
in nothing but his overalls
we warmed each other with
hugs the best we could

Words coming to me the way
they do when I least
expect them

All of a sudden
I knew
my mom
was
hoping
while we
were
hunkering
down
there

the wind
would
blow
our
Nebraska
farm
away

GOING TOO FAR

Our English teacher falls asleep in class
Right in the middle of a sentence
suddenly his head nods & he is out
No one moves or makes a sound
because we know
when he wakes it will be with a start
Inside his head a roaring
a growling like a bear
sprung from hibernation

So we sit, frozen in our seats
longing to leap up
& run from the room
but we do not dare

Today Lidia leans across the aisle
offers me a piece of gum
& I take it & smile
stick it in my notebook to chew later
write, *Thank you*
& point to it so I can't be caught
passing a note
an offense punishable with
Mr. Borden's paddle

She writes back a word on paper, whispers
That's Anishinaabemowin for "you're welcome"

I try the syllables under my breath
ask for another new word
She points me to one phrase after another
until we forget the necessary care

Sprung from some dung heap
Mr. Borden grabs her by the
front of her blouse and pushes her
feet dangling, against the classroom wall
When I rise to try & stop him
someone holds the back of my sweater
tugs me down
In the seat behind me, Joey Redfern
shakes his head no, whispers,
It will be worse for her if you do.

WHEN GRAMPS ASKS

I raced home to tell Gram & Gramps about it
forgetting for a minute my mom was there
I raced home to tell them
what Mr. Borden did to Lidia
in class today
when it was both of us
passing words
back and forth across the aisle
and something else I saw
right before the buses came
Lidia in a corner by the storeroom door
crying, her hair a mess
her face already bruising in ways
that classroom slamming shake
couldn't have done

I ran to help her but
she pushed me away
stumbled out to catch
the bus, eyes cast down
a whimper in her throat
I don't think she could control

Stood there watching her
saw her curl up in the seat
behind the Ojibwe driver
saw the terrible look he gave me
like this was all my fault
and the doors closed
and the bus rolled away

But at supper when Gramps asked
Anything exciting happen at school today?
the way he does every night

I gave one panicked glance at Mom
then bent my head
and used my mouthful of mashed potatoes
to mumble, *Nothing much* . . .

LIDIA'S EMPTY SEAT
IN ENGLISH CLASS

Lidia hasn't been back to school
I watch every morning
as the kids tumble off
the bus from Onigum
Maybe I could catch her
I'm thinking, before she goes to class
ask her how she is, if she's all right

Her empty seat in English class
is like a loud yell
and when Mr. Borden speaks
I want to holler, *Gibaakwa'an gidoonish!*
what Lidia said meant
Shut your damned mouth
when she was trying to teach me
to speak Anishinaabemowin

I even asked Joey Redfern
if he knew where she was
but he said no
I don't know why
but I didn't believe him
I think he knows something
he just won't say.

THE SECOND
BIG BLIZZARD

It's a deep snow December
so we tied a rope from Gram's willow
to the birch to our back door
That's so we can hang onto it as we go from
our Little House to the Big House & back
at night if the path is drifted shut
if snow is blowing so hard
we can't see two feet in front of us
and not worry
about stepping down into ten
twelve feet of soft new snow
filling the gully where it drops off neat
behind the birch tree.

THERE ARE ALWAYS STORIES AROUND THE LITTLE STOVE

It was Mom who told the story tonight
to Gram & Gramps while I was doing my homework
in the next room
how in the hospital bed right after his surgery
Daddy sharing his room with a funny little man
sunken in, Mom said, with cancer so far gone
the man's family bent on
putting him through another round of radiation
How my dad spoke up when the man couldn't
said, *All he wants is to go home . . .*
And the woman asked, *Is that true, Pop?*
and the man could only nod
while tears raced one another
down the furrows of his face
Mom said Daddy wouldn't sleep
until he knew the people understood

Mom told Gram & Gramps all about it
how Daddy did that even at a time
when hope was still foremost in his heart
how the man thanked him
the day his family came
to take him home.

AT NIGHT I DREAM ABOUT WHAT
MR. BORDEN DID

I see Mr. Borden holding Lidia by the front of her blouse
slamming her against that wall
her whole weight suspended in his
clutching right hand
the up down of her hitting the bulletin board
until fabric ripped
and he dropped her like she was
nothing but
a sack of wild rice

But she was Lidia, so she
pressed her lips into one hard firm line
I saw tears rise in her gray eyes
and then recede
in what I knew was an act of will

And when I wake up I lie there, burning with shame
thinking how we all sat like frozen lumps
how by rights Mr. Borden should have
grabbed me, too, but he didn't

How I should have tried to stop him
but I didn't & it wasn't just because
Joey Redfern held onto the back of my sweater
& wouldn't let it go

The other students in that classroom
I saw how their eyes glazed over
before falling down to their desktops
willing themselves invisible
in case Mr. Borden's spell hung on

And we all sat there like that
all of us white kids
when we knew to our toenails
Mr. Borden wouldn't dare
to lay a hand on a one of us

Hackensack greasers &
reservation Indians
Now, that's another story.

MY FATHER WAS A QUIET MAN

I wish I had a letter from my dad
one I could read over and over
to hear his voice behind
the written words
but Daddy wasn't much for writing
always said he left that
up to my mother
and me
so I've only got the one note
I saved, one he'd scribbled on a lined tablet
telling me to use the money he sent
to buy Mom birthday gifts
how much he missed us
seemed like the summer
would never end

The note is too short to hear his voice
but I'm glad I kept it
because he's in it just the same

My dad was a quiet man
till he was riled
and when he was
he spoke out, his big body
and big voice
like exclamation marks
for what he said

There are times
you've got to, Sweet Pea
whether you want to or not . . .

That's Daddy's voice

something you've just got to do

Those are Daddy's words
raising a ruckus every day now
inside my head.

THEN LAST NIGHT I DREAMED
ABOUT TUCK

He looked exactly like you'd expect him to
if he had lived, if he had gone on
and grown up right alongside me

In the dream he was
mad at me
he said, *I'd never let something like that*
happen to you and not say something
to someone . . .

Then that made me mad and I said
Who are you to talk? You're dead . . .

And he said, *Maybe it's time for you*
to be the boy
which made no sense whatsoever
and I started to cry
and woke up
but my pillow was dry so I knew
I wasn't really crying
any more than Tuck was really there
being my brother, telling me
what he thought I ought to do.

I CAN'T TALK
TO MY MOM ABOUT IT

She's all the time sitting
in the kitchen nook
staring out the window
at the snow

And when I interrupt her
she grabs my chin hard
cranks it toward her
twisted-up face, shouts
*Allie Benton, what's
the matter with you?*

Then she lets me go
sits staring out the window
and forgets all over again
I'm even there

I can't talk to my mom
when she's fidgeting over
the way Kitsy howls at night
after she's shut him up
down there in the basement

or when she looks
right through me
like I'm one of the ghosts
constantly haunting

our house these days.

MY WORDS LINE UP TO SPEAK

I want to be like my dad
but I'm not
My voice creaks out
cracks & quivers
and in my head
my words line up to speak
but when I open my mouth
they come out all garbled instead

I want to do like Tuck
tells me in my dreams
but fear shivers my knees
turns my insides
to slivered ice

and I walk on past
the principal's office

again.

WHAT I DID WAS, I WROTE A LETTER

So, what I did was, I wrote a letter
to Mr. Walter, the principal

A very short letter
Mailed it at the post office
when no one was there to see me do it

Dear Mr. Walter, it said
I am in Mr. Borden's ninth grade English class
and I have to report his extreme
physical discipline of Lidia White Cloud
the week after Thanksgiving.
What he did had to be against the law
and I don't understand why
nothing is ever done to stop him.
Someone said it's because he only
beats up on the Indian kids and maybe that's true
but it still doesn't make it right.

At first I didn't sign my name
too scared, what they would do to me

but then I thought about Lidia
the way she leaned over
& shared her words
with me

So I went ahead & signed it

A concerned student, Allie Benton.

FIRST CHRISTMAS WITHOUT MY DAD

It's nearly Christmas so
Gramps put a family of dead stuffed deer
out on our lawn in the snow
and we hung cranberries & popcorn
on a small pine for the birds

Mom refuses to cut a young tree
for anything, so Gramps says
We'll just have Christmas
out here on the hill

Last year my dad bought presents
put them under the TV
Mom didn't give in about the tree
but later a pine bough, some holly
& a red candle appeared

My dad just smiled

At the last possible minute
I decide to wrap up a smoked whitefish
a jar of Gram's plum jam
& a poem I wrote

At the post office I used the end of
my birthday money & sent it to
            Lidia White Cloud
            Onigum, Minnesota
If it doesn't come back I hope
that means she got it.

A HATRED OF CATS

The air smelled of snow again
the day Kitsy disappeared

Mom said she's sure
Kris Svedstrom took him
drove out to the country
dropped him and drove away

Because of their bird feeders, she said
and the way they hate cats

I haven't slept for days and look at
the Svedstroms differently now

This is much worse than
that long ago summer when
Kris tore the heads off
my favorite paper dolls.

LAST DAY OF SCHOOL BEFORE CHRISTMAS BREAK

Joey Redfern stopped by my locker
I was leaning over
tugging on my boots
ready to leave for home

I heard what you did
he said

and I stopped tugging
wracked my brain for what
in the world
he was talking about

For Lidia
he said

I thought he meant the dumb
present I sent her

Wow, he said
*I can't believe you wrote a letter
to Mr. Walter*

How did he know that?
No one else has said a word

Wow, he said again
*I can't believe you did that
for Lidia . . .*

and he walked with me
all the way down
the hill from school.

SOMETIMES THAT MEANS
TELLING LIES

On Christmas Day we go to Aunt Ida's for dinner
She has high blood pressure so she cooks
without salt & her food tastes like cardboard
especially her pumpkin pie

Mom says we have to be thankful
Sometimes that means telling lies

The only real test of success in a woman
is if she bears a boy child, I hear Gram
telling childless Aunt Ida. *If she*
bears a boy child & keeps him alive . . .

How long? Aunt Ida asks from her
embroidery. *Keeps him alive how long?*

Gram's eyes light on my mother

Longer than the girl child
she says pointedly

Mom's eyes meet mine

There I am, still alive, across the room.

ON THE SUNDAY AFTER CHRISTMAS

Gram fixes fried chicken
Aunt Ida comes to dinner at three
Gramps walks her home
before dark

Then the four of us play
Chinese checkers
on his hand-carved wooden board

Gram cheats at checkers, too.

IT'S A NEW YEAR, BUT NO LIDIA

All day long our first day back
I kept hoping Lidia would show up
Maybe she's late, I thought, and caught a ride

The intercom crackled in homeroom
announcing that Mr. Borden was out sick

In English class I kept thinking
Maybe Lidia'll show up now & be glad
to see there's a substitute

I thought, maybe she'll be in home ec

She's never been in algebra with me
she says that's because
All us Indians
get stuck in dummy math

But the day ended
No Lidia

No Joey Redfern either so
I walked down the hill alone.

IN GYM CLASS TODAY

Right in the middle of a failed
forward roll while I was
upside down on the mat
just before I sprawled
flat on my back
I heard Ardis whispering
to Christine
That terrible Mr. Borden . . .
but Mrs. Bakke stopped her
before I could hear
the rest

And in the locker room
rushing to towel dry
after our showers
they were whispering again
& this time Bonnie joined in, said
*My mom told me that's just
not true . . .*

And that time I wanted to
straighten up & say
right out loud
*What are you talking about?
What do you know?*

But these are the girls
who never speak to me
who never even look at me
unless it's to giggle or laugh

And all I know is that it's been
weeks now and Mr. Borden's
not back, but no one's said a word
to me about my letter
except Joey & I still don't know
how or what he knows.

DEPRESSION COOKIES

After school Gram & I make Depression Cookies
Mom calls them that 'cause back in the 1930s
during the Great Depression when there
wasn't enough flour or sugar or eggs
for cookies or cake
Gram used to use the last of her powdered sugar
to make butter frosting so they could
spread it between saltine crackers
call them cookies, call it *making do*

We're spreading frosting when out of nowhere
Gram chuckles & says, *I heard some*
really good letter writer
helped Ted Borden
get bed rest behind bars . . .

My shoulders tighten & my hands start to shake
but I keep my eyes down & don't say a thing

Gram goes on, *John Walter's keeping quiet*
who the student was, but I figure it
had to be someone in the ninth grade . . .

I pop a saltine on top of a cracker already
thick with frosting, shove the whole thing
in my mouth & shrug at Gram
glad for once that Mom's over there
at the Little House, staring at the walls.

NOT ANYMORE THEY'RE NOT

Well, Gram says, shooting me another
shrewd look, *I sure would like to congratulate*
whoever wrote that letter . . .
I hope they keep the bastard in that sanitarium
a good long time!

I pop another stack of frosting & crackers
in my mouth & let Gram see
how she's made me grin

She gives in then, says
I don't know why your grandfather
turns up his nose
at these Depression Cookies

I like 'em better than the real thing . . .

I do, too. And I don't think I'll ever
call them Depression Cookies again.

MY LETTER TO LIDIA

My letter to Lidia is short
& to the point

My gram says Mr. Borden is gone for good
so it's probably safe
for you to
return to school

I'll tell you all about it
when you get here

Please come back

Your niijikwe, Allie

And I ran with it
all the way
to the post office

and, unable to stop
running even then
I ran without it
all the way
back home.

AN EMBARRASSMENT OF RICHES

In our Christmas parcel from Uncle Wayne & Aunt Lulu
my cousin Trudy sent me two of her skirts
ones she wore last year and can't wear now
They fit fine if I roll them over
at the waist
One's black and the other is
dark gold with brown & red plaid
Between blizzards, Mom & I
went to Bemidji shopping
At O'Meara's she bought me three sweaters
with knee socks & roll-down socks
to match each one

Mom says if your socks match your top
it looks like an outfit
no matter what's in between

With Trudy's skirts & my new sweaters
I can make six different
combinations and with Friday being
jeans day at school, even if I just wear slacks
that means I've got outfits for a week & a half
without having to repeat myself

Gram says it's an *embarrassment of riches*
Gramps says it's a *darned good math lesson*
And Mom says, *We'll get you one more sweater
when Daddy's first social security check comes*

I hold my breath, hoping after that
she'll buy me jeans.

MAKING DO

Lidia rolls her eyes at my new outfit
I can tell by the twist of her lips
she's about to say something snide
but then she has a coughing fit
& can't stop till she's crying

What're you coming to school with wet hair
in January for? I ask her, just like it's not
her first day back, just like it's not
the first chance we've had to talk

And then I rush on before she can cuss at me

Hey, I say, gathering up my courage
to go on, *my mother always says, Don't go out*
in winter with a wet head or you'll catch
Instant Pneumonia & die

I suppose she recites examples
of people who died instantly of it
Lidia says, coughing again like crazy

The sound of her cough scares me
Cover your head, Mom says, even if
I dried my hair. Your pores are open . . .
Open pores are where

Instant Pneumonia spores get in
Lidia pitches in, *Body heat activates them*

Like boiling water on Minute Rice, I add
And I'm laughing to cover how glad I am
she's there, we're there talking again, *Yup*
They hit your brain and bam! You're dead

Tears roll off Lidia's high cheekbones
& splash off her chin
I pass her a handful of cough drops
and we lean on each other in the hallway
laughing harder

For a minute or two we both forget
how impossible people make it
for us to be friends.

IN HOME EC TODAY

Lidia got sick & had to leave
Mrs. Leland let me help her
down to the nurse's office
but the nurse wouldn't let me stay
so I didn't see Lidia again
till she was bundled onto the school bus
and heading home

Wouldn't you know it was
Christine & Ardis in home ec who
tried to broil cheese toast
& burned the cheese
so bad you could smell it
all over school

It made *me* want to heave
but I didn't

Lidia sure did, though
She lost it all over the floor
just before she got to the exit
where she puked her guts out
again in the snow
& again
in the hall on her way
to see the nurse

Between her cough that
won't go away
& her weak stomach
she really ought to go to
the doctor

Her skin today
usually so clear
& beautiful
was clearly green.

THE THIRD BIG BLIZZARD

If you put plastic over windows on the outside
& masking tape the cracks inside
if you tape shut the front door facing north
roll cloth into bottom gap &
shove rugs against it all

If you draw shades & close curtains
you can't see out but then
the only place
the wind comes in
is through
the walls . . .

It's too cold in the basement
to use the bathroom
but we have to flush the toilet daily
to keep the pipes from freezing
The toilet seat's so cold
I tell Mom it creates
Instant Constipation
and she shakes her head, laughing
When it's this cold
we're forced to take a chamber pot
upstairs at night . . .

When this blizzard died down
after a day & a half
of snow & wind the back door had
drifted shut, our only winter exit

Gramps began to shovel through
from the Big House but the snow
was three, four feet deep in places

I climbed out our bedroom window
hanging onto the sill till I was sure
the crust would hold me

Then I got another shovel
& went to help Gramps.

NOT LISTENING TO MY MOTHER,
PRETENDING I DON'T HEAR

My mother always says
Don't put toilet paper in the toilet
That's what the paper bag
that's lining the trash can's for
And don't flush every time
you use it, either
what a waste of water
Flush every other or every few
or when the water gets too yellow

I don't care what they do
at the Svedstroms' house
We're not the Svedstroms
Are we the Svedstroms?
You want to be the one who
cleans up the mess when the
cesspool backs up
to kingdom come?

I didn't think so . . .

Don't dump the slop pot
in broad daylight
in full view of the road
What will the neighbors think
for heaven's sake?
Besides which, it's unsanitary

Of course, your grandma says
that's why Gramps's tomatoes
grow so huge
Oh, she's just fooling
Most of the time she takes it
to the outhouse

If she didn't, what would
the neighbors say?

Always wear a nightgown
It gives them something to take off
They like looking underneath
They prefer not knowing
going under and then knowing
Never being sure

Mother! I say, *Come on . . .*

No, it's true
You've got to leave some mystery
Wear a nightie, she says
eyes twinkling
Wear a nightie
over nothing.

EVER SINCE THE DAY WE WALKED
DOWN THE HILL

Joey follows me to my locker
& stands there while I change books
& then he walks me to biology

One time when I looked up from
dissecting a frog
he was staring at me &

I could feel my face turn ten shades of red.

WHAT IF LIDIA DIED

It's two weeks since the last big blizzard
& Lidia hasn't been here
even one day
What if she died of that awful cough she had
What if Mom was right
& she came down with
Instant Pneumonia
or food poisoning
or something
& out there at Onigum
there wasn't one person who could
save her

There's no one to ask except Joey Redfern
The Ojibwe girls don't speak to me
not even when I walk right up to them
& shaking in my boots
manage to spit out my words

I ask Gramps if he'll take me out there
to where Lidia lives . . .
he just shakes his head & says
No he doesn't
think that's a good idea

I don't dare ask my mom.

MY MOTHER KEEPS A SCARY HOUSE

If you wake up in the middle of the night
with stomach pains
it probably means
you're going to die
Run for Dr. Ridley
See if he'll come
If he won't, chew Rolaids
shiver and pray out loud
Eventually you'll fall asleep
If you wake up in the morning
like he says
more'n likely you aren't dead . . .

Our family has a history of nervous disorders
Mom says, morning after
she's had me up all night
I'm in the kitchen nook
drinking coffee
studying fast & hard
for a history test
where all the facts have
been chewed to bits
by a long night
of Mom's teeth-chattering fears
Grandpa's shaking, she continues
my spells, your Uncle Jake . . .

Something to watch out for
she says. *Probably*
it'll happen to you, too

I hate history.

OTHER THINGS I HATE

I hate how small this house is
with no hot water
no bathtub or shower
the way we have to sponge bathe
in the kitchen at night
with the lights off

not having a phone

I hate eating nothing but venison
& wild rice. Canned green beans
I want hamburger & fried chicken again
French fries

I hate having to share a bedroom
with my mother
how our twin beds end to end
fill up the room
the head of my bed at her feet

I hate how cold the toilet seat is
no matter when we use it
The chamber pot with its
icy metal rim, its smell
Dumping & cleaning it
every single day

I hate washing clothes by hand
& hanging them to dry
over the metal furnace grate
I hate furnace duty, the way it breaks sleep
in the middle of every other night

But what I hate the most is waking up
in the cold dark center of a sound sleep
to hear my mother sobbing in her bed next to mine
as if she is the only one who will ever be
allowed to miss my father, my brother
as if she is the only one missing the life
we all used to have together.

I DON'T THINK
THE SVEDSTROMS DID IT

I don't think they stole Kitsy
and left him, as sweet, soft
& purring as he was, to die

More likely it was some semi
got him on the highway
or maybe a freight train

He'd freeze out there alone
I tell my mom

That image haunts me

I don't think the Svedstroms
would do that.

IT'S LIKE A ZOO HERE

In at the Big House back door
a deer & a moose loom while
a mean-looking badger mother hisses
at a raccoon in Gramps's studio

To get to the living room
you've got to pass
a bobcat poised to pounce
& a big old grizzly bear
rearing up on hind legs
all mouth & teeth & claws

The top of Gram's piano
is lined with mallard ducks,
a loon & a stuffed owl

They'll all end up in Uncle Jake's
museum trailer eventually

But right now, this winter
it's like a zoo in here
with all the animals
stuffed & ready

and living with us.

MOM GOT A JOB AT THE HOTEL

The pay is lousy, Mom says
She works three-thirty to ten so I eat supper
with Gram & Gramps, do my homework there
At least we can have a hamburger
every once in a while now

We're sick to death
we're sick to death
we're sick to death
of venison & smoked fish

With her first paycheck
Mom sent in the catalog
for two pairs of jeans
& they came yesterday

They fit real good

She got me new fur-lined boots
& four pairs of warm socks, too.

YESTERDAY FOR A CHANGE

Mom was in a good mood so
she brought a six-pack of beer
& leftover fried chicken
home from the hotel

Ten-thirty on a school night
reading romance comic books
eating chicken & drinking beer
we're giggling like we're both fourteen
not just me

Don't get grease on the pages
she reminds me over & over between giggles
I have to take them back tomorrow . . .

BUT TODAY IS A BAD DAY

And on a bad day
our Little House knows
before door slam what we're in for

A Mom tirade, Mom rampage
Mom on a what-am-I-alive-for
long-hauling-slug-beneath-the-belt assault

I don't say anything but she shouts,
Your father would roll over in his grave
if he could hear you sass

Then she throws herself
on her knees by the bed
Give me strength, she hollers
praying to the heavens
Give me strength & a better daughter!

I don't ask her
Do you mean the one
you have on a good day . . .

I don't suppose she does.

I WON THE REGIONAL SPELLING BEE

And I got to go to State
In Minneapolis they
eliminated me
on the word
elegiac
after the first round

Those Catholic schools
Mom declared
It's inhuman the way
they grill those kids . . .

Then she took me shopping
& to the Nankin
for Chinese

My first period came
at the hotel the night of
the big spelling bee banquet
and I was scared

Mom went to get me
what I needed and
demonstrated
what to do

Don't be scared, she said
They call it a curse
but it's really a miracle.

ANOTHER LETTER WRITTEN & SENT

I wrote Lidia another letter
from Minneapolis
I'm not sure why

Something about
my mom being
so nice &
understanding
for a change
got me remembering
Lidia's words about her mother
that she read that day
It seems like such a long
long time ago

I didn't tell her that

But I did tell her school
was awful without her
& about the spelling bee
& how I messed up
on such an easy word

And I told her
we still had a substitute teacher
in English, how glad I was
it looked like
Mr. Borden wasn't coming back

And I told her
I wished she'd write me
just one letter
letting me know
what she was doing
if she was okay.

PRETTY ENOUGH

Every year my mother & I
watch Miss America on TV
and when they're taking
that long judgment walk
she sighs & says
Your cousin Trudy could be
Miss America, you know . . .

Then she waits for me to agree
before she goes on
She's pretty enough
& with her personality
she could be Miss America
she really could

Am I pretty? I ask my mom
At fourteen
it's mirror mirror on the wall
and I want fairest

There is a long pause

You're at<u>trac</u>tive, she says
stressing the <u>trac</u>
You're inter<u>est</u>ing, she says
stressing the <u>est</u>

Not pretty, I think
but do not say

I want to be pretty.

MAYBE WE COULD

There's only one boy at school
who makes me laugh out loud
right in the middle of class

Yesterday he sat beside me in assembly
and right before we stood up to pledge
allegiance to the flag, his leg moved
It bumped up against mine
The funniest feeling ran up & down my spine

I looked at him sideways
not moving my head
and this time he was the one blushing

I like him
It seems like we could
maybe be friends
I wonder if my mom would let me
I wonder.

YOU CAN'T

You can't go out with Joey Redfern
His mother's an Indian
and nobody knows who
his father is
Some say it's the banker
but to tell the truth
he looks more like the baker
It doesn't matter which white man
You can't go out with Joey Redfern

He's an Indian.

WHAT DIFFERENCE DOES IT MAKE?

I had to ask her
*What difference does it make
that he's an Indian?*

And she started in raving
about *the pathway to destruction
the road to hell*

I don't know what my dad
would have said
about me dating
an Indian

but I do know that
today I decided
to go to hell.

THE ROAD TO HELL

He lives in town, not out on the reservation
His mom works at the post office
I don't know where his dad is unless
what Mom said about him is true
All I know is, he's got six sisters
and they are every last one of them
giving me looks at school

I asked him to March Madness
because that's the dance where girls ask boys
only I told my mother it was
just a bunch of us
going together
and with his sisters
that turned out to be true, too

When we danced I wanted him to pull me close
but he didn't and when the dance was over
I wanted him to walk me home alone
but the whole gang came along

He says next weekend if the ice holds
we can go skating
if he can get away without
all of his sisters
finding out & raising hell

I think he likes me, 'cause
instead of calling him Joey
like everyone else does
he asked me to
call him Joe.

CAT SENSE

Kitsy came back
having survived winter
but he's wild now
Every day he comes right
to the edge of the lawn
and meows at me
but he won't come closer

I've noticed when Mom's there
he won't come at all.

A REALLY WEIRD THING
HAPPENED TODAY

The home ec teacher, Mrs. Leland
caught me in the hallway
& gave me a note
Lidia had written to me

It said, *Allie, I can't come back*
to school anymore
I'm going to have a baby
and I'm getting married
I'm sorry we can't be friends
Be careful who you run with
  Lidia
P.S. Joe told me what you did
  Miigwech, niijikwe

I asked Mrs. Leland how she got the note
but she just shrugged and walked away

All day I've been wondering
who Lidia's going to marry
She didn't even have a boyfriend
when she was in school

And a baby

I guess if she's getting married that means
she'll get to keep it

None of this makes sense

If she had a telephone
I'd try to call her
if we had a telephone, too.

GRAMPS TOLD
THE STORY LAST NIGHT

Mom was still at the hotel
Gram downstairs washing dishes
Gramps on his creaky leather stool
beside the little space heater
chewing tobacco & spitting
into a Folger's can

If you've got to get to Onigum in April
Gramps said, *cross the bay but*
take a board
He was talking about the time
he & Kris's grandfather
had to get to Onigum for some business deal
but the roads were out, slick & deep
with mud

Five foot maybe six foot long
that board, Gramps said. *It's a bitch to carry*
but you'll need it
for the bigger cracks
in the ice
where the floes
have separated
and are floating free . . .

Gramps said Old Grandpa Svedstrom told them
It'll be a miracle if you young fools
make it back!

Did you ever do it? I asked
& Gramps nodded. Chewed for a minute
shook his head & spit into the can

Tell someone you're going, he said
and take a board . . .

I DON'T KNOW
WHAT MADE ME DO IT

But I decided to go
Hell-bent on getting to Onigum
So I asked Joe if he wanted to come
He knows where Lidia lives
I can't stop thinking about her
especially since Mrs. Leland
gave me Lidia's note

Gramps won't take me out there
I want to see where she lives
maybe see one of those grave houses
like they made for her mother

See her

We only got halfway
& then the cracks were so big
we had to turn back
Behind us the ice creaked & groaned
Ahead of us we could hear it shivering
into new cracks, small highways of dark water
waiting for the least mistake
as we headed one slow step at a time
back to town

Safe again on shore
we swore each other to secrecy
Joe said he'd have to be boiled alive
for anyone to force that out of him
Stupid as it was what we did.

WHAT JOE KNOWS

Even though no one knows who his father is
and his mom's family all lives up at Red Lake
on the closed reservation
where the Indian kids all go to school
just with each other
instead of coming to town school
with the white kids
Joe knows
how to play football & basketball
how to play baseball & chess
how to play a guitar
how to get good grades
how to make great speeches
how to drive a speedboat
& how to get town kids to like him even though
he's as much Ojibwe as most of the kids
out at Onigum

and . . .

even though he lives in town
& his mom works at the post office
& all his sisters hang out with
each other & other town girls
Joe knows
how to hunt & fish

how to trap muskrats & trade their fur
how to shoot a .22 & a shotgun
how to kill a deer
how to fish & how to clean the fish
& how to cook it over the campfire he knows
how to build from scratch
how to paddle a canoe

& how to tease his sisters so
they won't tell his mom he's with me

& how to kiss a girl so she
wants him to kiss her again or at least
that's what I've heard

I won't write it down here that
anyone heard it from me.

EVEN JOE SAYS

Leave it alone

I know he means Lidia, what I do
wondering how she is all the time
what's going on with her
wanting to see her
not being able to figure out
where the boyfriend
came from
or who he is

Leave it alone, Joe says

And it's like that time
he pulled on the back
of my sweater
Held me down

With the strength
of his insistence
held me down

What makes this division?
Indian
White
reservation
town

And what about Mr. Borden?

Gram says he's home now
but she heard he'll
never be able to teach

I'm not sure I believe that
I think if it's let alone long enough
they'll all forget

& he'll be back again.

A CAPABLE WOMAN

Mom replaced the pipes under the kitchen sink
They burst one night when temperatures dropped
so low & the furnace went out we slept so hard
I thought sure Mom would be hysterical
but she was gleeful instead

If they'd burst in the ground, she says
we'd have had to move in with Gram & Gramps
for the rest of the winter

With the attic boarded up, I say

Drawing straws, she says, laughing
who sleeps with Grandma, who gets the couch

You know how to do this? I ask & hold my breath

Not much in this line I don't know how to do
she says, lining up a gasket & tightening it with a wrench
Your father so inept with his hands, she says
but matter-of-fact

A more capable woman than your mother
you'll never find, I remember Daddy saying
Pay attention how she does things

There is nothing she sets her mind to
that woman can't do. Especially
she's working with her hands

And he held out his, stretching thick
brown fingers their full length
These hands, he said. *Good for growing things*
Or piloting a tugboat against a wicked river current
through the center of a whirlpool . . .

I see those hands now. Good for lifting & holding
Good for tucking covers around sleep's edges
Good for holding a small girl steady
walking against a rough spring wind
And, yes, I see

Having a capable mother when she's pretty near
all I've got left, can be a good thing, too.

WILL THE REAL GRAM PLEASE STAND

Mom snapped first
then Gram & Mom both
slammed doors

Sometimes I hate my mother
Mom said

And I wondered if she
had any idea
how most days I feel about her
same way she feels about Gram.

THERE'S A NEW GIRL IN SCHOOL

Moved here so late she can't be in band either
so she got stuck in 9-B with me
In home ec she knows
how to cook anything
Mrs. Leland gives us
but she says she'd rather not
In math she freezes
& the teacher calls her
a dumb blonde
but she says, *Who cares?*

Her name is Beth
& I think
maybe
we're going to be friends.

NEW MOON NIGHTS

All the boys are drawn to Beth
like bees to honey
like those crazy ants
running after sugar Gram puts down
But she's not boy crazy
She's just a lot of fun

After school today I went to her house
supposedly to sew . . .
we've got vests to do for home ec
and her mom's got a sewing machine

But first we went to Louden's Café

Because it was Beth,
a bunch of boys tagged along
Doug showed me how to stick a bread knife
up a table jukebox slot till coins roll out
& you can play songs for hours
on the same quarter

It was dark by the time we walked to Beth's house
just past Trott's yard, right on the lakeshore

Dave & Kris joined us at the library
all seven of us running crack the whip
down the center of the street
all of us laughing & shouting

Up above, a dark spring sky filled with stars
one thin slice of new moon
way more wish than promise.

EVEN MORE THINGS
I DON'T TELL MOM

I don't tell her how much I like Beth
She's different from the other girls
Maybe it's because she lived in a big city
before they moved here
or because they moved around a lot
She's even lived in California

At her house nobody tells us what to do
except her dad if he's home drunk
I don't tell my mom that
or about the way her mother uses a
Ouija board & lets us play, too

The only time I don't like Beth
is when I forget & talk about Lidia

Last time she turned up
the music real loud
& said, *What do you want to
talk about* her *all the time for?*

I wonder if she's jealous
or if in this one thing
she's just like everyone else
looking down her nose at Lidia
because she's an Indian.

UP IN GRAM'S ATTIC

Beth & I spent all day Saturday pulling boxes
out from under the attic eaves
We found a box filled with old dresses
& with them a bag of hats

Those are your mother's, Gram says
You better ask her if you
can play with them . . .

Mom said, *Sure . . . go put them on*

When we were dressed
Gram said, *Aren't you a picture?*
And Mom sat down at the piano
I always thought was Gram's alone
& where church songs were all I thought
anyone could play & all of a sudden
Mom's fingers flew over the keys

Some wild & crazy music was witching
everywhere . . .

Beth & I tried to kick & twirl, the way
you see people do in old movies
but we couldn't get our feet & legs
to match what we remembered of the mood

Mom grabbed Gramps & began to dance
& Gram slid in & began to play . . .

It didn't last long, only a song
or two, but it was wild
the way Mom spun & whirled
kicked & twirled till she was out of breath
& so were we

That was fun! Beth said
when Gram & Mom
had gone back to the kitchen
& Gramps was painting again
and she's right, it was

fun.

WHITE TRASH LIKE RIVER RATS

Maybe it's good I got used to being called a river rat
back in Nebraska, 'cause now words & looks & snubs
run right off me like rain off a slicker
one of those bright yellow shiny things
my mother used to make me wear

It would make my dad sad
the way kids in school call names
make judgments

Even Beth asked me today
Why don't you go out with a white boy
instead of some Indian?

I got up and walked right out of
Louden's Café, but then there was
no place to go but home

Gramps asked how come
I was back so early
Gram asked what was wrong
Mom didn't ask anything
'cause she wasn't there
She was working like she mostly always is

I didn't tell them someone in school today
wrote WHITE TRASH all over my locker
in black marker pen
the kind that you can rub till it blurs
but it won't wash off

At first I thought it was Onigum girls
how they look at me like Joe
is their property
but lately they've been nicer

one girl even smiled.

I CAN'T BELIEVE IT HAPPENED

Joe gave me his ring today
right after school, but
before basketball practice

Standing by our lockers
he asked me
Will you wear it?

I said I would & I did
I wore it
all the way home
with a strip of paper
wrapped around it
so it would fit

And then I hung it
on a chain inside my sweater
the way the other girls do

It's a secret, the kind I'd like to share
with a girlfriend

Wish I still had one.

TODAY AT THE FIVE & DIME

Joe & I stopped on our way home
from school today
to buy gum & licorice Snaps
and on our way out the door
we ran into Lidia coming in

She walked right past me
and I said, *Lidia . . .*
and she kept walking
down the aisle by the nail polish
& fake fingernails and I said
Lidia again, this time louder
and she stopped

There was a woman with her
Joe told me later it was her Aunt Mary
and the woman kept on walking
down the aisle and then
down the steps to the basement
where they keep the fabric
& sewing supplies

Lidia pulled her coat tight around her
before she turned to talk to me
She looked embarrassed
and something else
I've never seen her cheeks
get pink like that
so sudden
and her eyes not quite meeting mine

Are you okay? I asked & felt stupid
Yeah, she said. *You? Hey, Joey* . . .

When are you getting married? I asked
and I saw a look go between them
and she said, *Oh, pretty soon . . . Hey, gotta go
someone's waiting for me* . . .
& she hurried down the stairs
before I could say
one right thing like

I really miss you.

SPRING CLEANING

Over at the Little House Mom climbs the ladder
hoists storm windows off their moorings,
lowers them to the ground

I hand up a hammer & Mom pounds
a long sharp nail into a gutter loosened
by winter's heavy icicle pull

Suds splash against explosed glass & windows blink
in sudden sunlight, relieved as they are
of a winter's worth of smoke & dust & grime

Spring cleaning the Little House inside & out
top to bottom

Two peas in a pod, Gramps says
as he walks by on his way to
the smokehouse

Who? I shout back

You two, Gramps says, laughing
and then says it again, *my two girls
two peas in a pod.*

TWO PEAS IN A POD

Uncle Jake & Auntie Win used to holler
How're our two peas in a pod doing today?
whenever they came to visit
but they meant my brother & me

Daddy nicknamed us Nip & Tuck
right after we were born
Mom says it was because I cried nonstop
from morning to night but Tuck just
slept & lay so good, so still

That was before they knew he was sick
his heart born weak, the hole in it
getting bigger & bigger
But even after they knew
even after the surgeries that didn't work
the nicknames stuck

Gram says what happened back then was
I did all the crying for both of us
Gramps says using my lungs like that
helped make me strong

But a sad sound in his voice reminds me
of wind sighing through weeping willow leaves

Nobody calls me Nip now, I suppose I know why.

TUCK TRIED SO HARD

I remember how we saw the twister
& ran for the storm cellar
hid down there in that cold, dank, rooted place
while above us funnel cloud
broke all decibels of roar

An hour or more
we were down there
then up out of the bowels of earth
we came

Three days later Tuck took sick
wheezing & coughing
Pneumonia, Doc Gerring said
Set deep into his chest

Tuck tried so hard, but he couldn't shake it
not with his already damaged heart
and a week later he died

Doc Gerring said it was
a combination of heart & lung did it
brought on by dank earth, mold
& spores & odd dust
kicked up in all that wild
& frenzied wind

Mom always blamed the tornado
when she wasn't blaming Nebraska
the root cellar, or my dad

Seven years ago now
a long time to hold a grievance
against the weather.

MY MOTHER THINKS
SHE CAN BURN MEMORIES

Last night I wrote the words
Nip & Tuck over & over on my notebook
stuck together until they nearly filled the cover

Nip & Tuck   Nip & Tuck   Nip & Tuck

Left it lying on the sofa before dinner
and this morning getting ready for school
it was nowhere to be found

Mom's eyes were suspiciously red, though,
and when I got home this afternoon

a fire in the incinerator was burning all the garbage
turning it in a matter of minutes into white ash
too powdery even for a memory.

THERE'S ANOTHER STORY I TELL MYSELF SO I WON'T FORGET

How on Fridays Daddy'd come home from the river early
lather up at the kitchen sink
wash dirt & grease from hands & arms & face
with Lava soap, then head to the bathroom
to take a shower with it

Comin' with me, Sweet Pea?
he'd ask once he was squeaky clean
and we would get in his '57 Ford
and go downtown to the store

Pick out steaks, big, thick sirloins
mushrooms, green onions
ripe juicy tomatoes, corn on the cob
And from Safeway's freezer
a gallon of Neapolitan ice cream

At home Mom would be baking bread
three dozen sour cream sugar cookies
and two blueberry pies

I'd set the table, while Mom mashed potatoes
sliced tomatoes, fried onions & mushrooms
around steaks sizzling in her huge cast iron pan

At the table Daddy & I ate
while Mom talked about her day

When my brother, Tuck, was alive
he was rewarded for his ready smile, but now
I was rewarded for chewing & swallowing a steak
the size of Nebraska
complete with all the trimmings

Look at that little girl eat!
my father would holler
She eats just like a man!
And we'd tuck into that big meal
all tight, warm, full as a family

I play it over and over in my head
so I won't forget but at the same time
I'm trying hard not to remember it as
the Last Supper we ever had together.

FIRST WEIRD THING
THAT HAPPENED TODAY

Kris told me all the guys
in the locker room were saying
I was easy

If they mean what I think they mean
why would they say that?

The only person I can think to ask is Beth
but she and I still aren't speaking

or Joe

'cause I know he was in
the locker room
with them

If my mom ever finds out
I'm hamburger.

SECOND WEIRD THING
THAT HAPPENED TODAY

Joe kissed me in the hallway
by my locker
right after baseball practice

And I didn't like it
I don't know why, but

for the first time
I didn't like it at all

The third weird thing
I'd say was this . . .

I gave him back his ring
and said, *I'm tired of secrets*
I'm tired of lies

It just slipped out
I don't even know
what I meant

And then I ran home
all the way
my heart feeling like
it would explode

But I didn't cry

I think that would be
the fourth weird thing.

I'M GLAD IT'S ALMOST SUMMER

I'm sick of all these wagging tongues
and how my mother keeps asking me
Is something wrong?
like I'll fall apart any second
I am not the one known for
flying to pieces every chance I get

Plus I got a job, working in an office
at the chamber of commerce
getting paid a dollar an hour
to write a newsletter & type it up
on mimeo sheets & run it off
to answer the telephone
& give out resort information
& for taking over the powwow payroll
like Gramps used to do
on Saturday nights all summer long

Joe says I'd be better off waitressing
the tip money's so good
and he's right of course
that's what Beth's going to do

Beth & I are speaking again
but we're not best friends

How can we be
after all the things
she said before
about Lidia &
about me dating an Indian

I'm glad summer is almost here
I'm sick to death of school
I'm sick to death of everything.

ON MEMORIAL DAY
WE GO TO THE CEMETERY

The earth over Daddy's grave sprouts new grass
almost blends now with the rest
Gram pulls dandelions while Gramps digs holes
for the two pots of begonias I hold
   in one hand red for my father
   in the other white for my brother

Mom wanders away down the hill
and I can see from the way she hunches forward
the way her shoulders move
she is crying
I think, I should put these begonias down
and run to comfort her

But the truth is, I am tired of her tears
how they push mine deeper inside
until I can feel them pulsing in there
shouting to break free
like the Missouri flooding
the way it was that time right after Tuck died
we were driving his body home to Gram
driving Mom home, too, to see if Gramps
could put the broken pieces of her back together

It's pretty here in the cemetery
Tall jack pines sway in soft spring breeze
leaves on the birch trees just beginning to darken
all the oaks and maples already lush & green
Birds are back, singing from highest branches
and overhead fluffy clouds float across a powder blue sky

My brother's small life was so fragile
I'll bet he's glad his bones are resting here
But my father, he'd rather be by the Missouri River
with her muddy water seeping through
If he's here at all, it's to see us, my mother, me
Maybe he & Tuck are together right here near us, watching
wishing they could reach through some spirit door

like that sudden shaft of sunlight
warming my pale still-winter face.

I SEE HER FIRST, CLIMBING OUT
OF AN OLD BLUE CHEVY

Even with her belly filled with child
she is beautiful
She looks as saucy as ever, tossing fringed shawl
over her arm, beaded earrings swinging
down to her shoulders

I've got the clipboard & the sign-up sheet
so I stand there waiting for her to reach
the head of the line
Either she doesn't see me or she's
pretending not to
My face flushes hot so fast
I know it must be red as autumn maple
and my mind racing . . .

At school last month Mrs. Leland took me aside
said, *This is for your own good, Allie*
Let go of the idea of Lidia as a friend
The Ojibwe are not our kind
She is not your kind

I pressed her, fury rising in me
like that old Missouri in a spring rain
Must have pressed too hard, 'cause I got the flood

Her own cousin knocked her up, Mrs. Leland said
Walking around town proud as you please
Everyone and his grandfather's had their way with her
You best stay away

Joe told me a different story

He says it was Mr. Borden, our English teacher
what he did to Lidia that day
after he jammed her against the wall
after he gave her that black eye
& those twisting bruises on her arms
Joe says it wasn't enough for him
It's never enough for a white man, Joe says

Now she's at the head of the line
Lidia White Cloud, she says
and then she looks up
Her eyes are gray clouds now
filled with summer storm
There is a wall between us
thick & hot like humidity
tornado air I remember
from my father's sickroom

And I choke back the words
I want to say to her
Repeat, instead, her own
Lidia White Cloud, I say
Write it down
Lidia White Cloud: Dancer

SOMETIMES I FEEL SO STUPID

I never put it together
Mr. Borden beating up on Lidia
or the way she had to leave school
because she was
having a baby

I still wonder if Joe is right

Or if Joe's blaming this
on Mr. Borden
because he's white
the same way my mother
blames things on Joe
because he's Ojibwe

Sometimes I feel so stupid
the things I take for granted
the things I don't even see.

AND WHAT MAKES A BOY
SO SPECIAL ANYWAY?

I think about Tuck sometimes
what little I remember
seems like I should remember more

Sickly from the first, not like me
All of us always tiptoeing around
like he was one of those made-of-glass
knickknacks Gram keeps stacked
on little corner shelves Gramps builds

Maybe I'd miss him more if my mother
wasn't all the time fingering what little
there is left of him, if Gram didn't always
have to cry every time someone says his name

His name was Lawrence like my father

When we were babies we looked exactly alike
In the pictures you can't even tell which one
is a boy, which one a girl
And when we're five, I'm the one
wearing cowboy hat & boots & cap-shooting guns

Every night after supper, far back
as I can remember we'd climb up into
Daddy's lap, me on one side in the big chair
Tuck on the other. We'd share Daddy's pie
and read book after book after book until
Mom came to take Tuck to bed

Daddy taught us both to read
but it was me he taught to milk a cow
bait a fishhook, shoot a gun
After Tuck died Daddy taught me to
drive the pickup, steer his tugboat
& use a pitchfork to protect myself from
copperheads & water moccasins

My mother isn't like that, she hogs grief
won't let anyone who's left us really go
Gram says Mom can't see what's right
in front of her, the ones left behind to love
maybe who need love more.

WONDERING WHAT MY FATHER
WOULD THINK OF JOE

I know I like the way Joe ducks his head
when he smiles

One time back when we were
still going steady, he grabbed my hand
in a movie at school & held it
until the lights came on
and I could feel the
gentle pressure of his fingers
on my palm
for days

I've been missing him, too

Tonight I saw him down on the corner
under the streetlight
so I walked real slow
& when I got to the park
I turned in & went to sit down on the rocks
where the dock was all summer
They took it in last week

He followed me into the park
He put his arm around me
& when I turned to say something

I don't remember what
he kissed me, & then he kissed me again
& we kept kissing until my lips
were thick from kissing his

And then he walked me halfway home
& I ran the rest
ran hard to get my heart back racing
in a way my head could
understand

And this time I told my mother
where I'd been.

YOU CAN'T GO OUT WITH
JOEY REDFERN

It's bad enough he's an Indian
but he's Catholic, too
That whole mess of family
Pagan up to their eyebrows
worshipping all those
graven images
Fish on Fridays
and sermons in some
dead language
His father's some white guy
And his mother's got a statue
of Jesus right on her dashboard

A town Indian &
Catholic on top of that . . .
I told you before, you can't
go out with Joey Redfern

Yes, I can.

COMING UP INTO THE LIGHT

You can only hunker down so long & then the wind dies
or rushes on to some other place to do its damage
& all that time you've been huddled there together
holding your breath, hoping against

wildest hope that up aboveground
nothing you love has been
blown away

hoping with a deep longing
the wind has cleared
the air &

the new
light
shining
is
there
to
stay

THE GHOST BOY

I told Joe tonight about the ghost boy
who walks beside me
all my days

and I showed him
some pictures of
me & Tuck
that last sad year
before the tornado struck
before he up & died

Joe said, *He looked*
just like you
and it hit me, that was
the first time anyone
ever said it that way round
not, *You look just like him*

I wonder what
my flesh & blood brother
would have thought of Joe

I'm pretty sure
the ghost boy
thinks he's just fine.

MISSING MY FATHER

My father comes closer to me in September, my birth time
that time when Nebraska corn waves giant leaves
six, seven feet off the ground

I can see Daddy striding down those rows, stopping
every now & then to finger an ear, breathe its scent
exclaim over ripe plumpness

One time I ran ahead of him, turned a corner
& couldn't find my way back. Tall as my father was
that Nebraska corn was taller. We had to holler

back and forth before he found me & when he did
he lifted me onto his shoulders so all the way back
to the truck, I was higher than the corn

Another time when I was with him in the Blue Moon Bar
I saw him pick a man up by his belt back, dangle him
upside down, held there in Daddy's big brown hands

Held there until the man said, *Sorry* in a convincing way
Sorry for how bad he was treating the woman
he came in there with

Last week my dad's family came to visit from Nebraska
Uncle Wayne brought river carp kept fresh on ice in a cooler
& Uncle Ray brought a projector, *Wait'll you see this, folks*

It was a movie of the last fish fry my dad was at out there
on the banks of the Missouri River. When I saw my dad
on the movie screen, walking down a sandy path to the boat

His bare brown arms swinging to match his stride
looking back over his shoulder, laughing
I thought I would have to swallow my heart

It rose to my throat & beat there with its own hard pounding
And for the first time since he died my tears flowed free
as the river he loved near as much as he loved

my mom, my brother, me.

MANAGING MY MOTHER

It's funny to me that my dad could speak up
with everyone except my mom
When he wanted something bad enough from her
he'd wait her out, say, *Now Maggie . . .*
smile & run long fingers through
his coal black hair, say, *Now Maggie*
another time & smile again, keep on
saying it & smiling until she gave in

Wish I could say I did it with his grace

Nowadays when my mother pitches a fit
like when she throws herself down hard
prays out loud or that time last week
she got so mad she threw a whole handful of silverware
at the front door, I stand there real still
& let a smile creep up around the edges of my lips

It's a crooked smile but it's the best I can do
& maybe it's crooked because most times
there's laughter lurking back there behind it

So I stick one hand on my hip & say
Oh Mom! How childish! or that last time I said
*Mom! What would Daddy say if he could
see you right now?*

What happens then is Mom gives in

Most times she runs to the bathroom, slams the door
cries loud enough for Svedstroms to hear
But when she comes out she says she's sorry
& that last time instead of running off
she stopped right there where she stood
in the middle of the Little House kitchen
looked at me like she was seeing me
for the first time

& then she threw her head back & laughed
Your daddy will never be dead as long as
you're alive, she said.

THAT'S HOW IT WORKED WITH JOE

I dug in my heels & hung on and now
Mom acts like she's the one invented him
And now my friends all say they like my mom
wish their moms were like her
the way she jokes & makes them laugh
how she trusts us & leaves us alone
now that it's okay for friends to come over

Beth says her mom never once talked to her
about stuff like getting her period or how to
get & keep a man or let her drink a beer
or have a glass of wine

Kris says how cozy & comfy our Little House is
how nice Mom keeps it, how much fun it is
to sit in the kitchen nook & play gin rummy
while Mom pops corn & dances along to the radio

Joe says he likes the way she knows how to
make him feel like a welcome guest
& every once in a while like he's home

When I hear them say it, I laugh & forget
the sound of silverware crashing against wood

I forget the way the door slams behind her
my mother's knees crashing down on wood floor

So to hear them talk makes me smile
and I think with a jolt of surprise it's my mom
they're talking about, my mom

And I think maybe they are seeing
some of the things my dad saw
that made him love her the way he did

And when I remember that even though
Joe's mom likes me, his grandma
won't let me come to their house

I think more of my mom &
for a minute I feel kind of proud.

I'M GLAD SCHOOL'S STARTED AGAIN

Mrs. Olaffson is our tenth-grade English teacher
and the first thing she did was give us each
a notebook, mine is blue, and say
*We're going to write in our journals
every single day*

I wanted to tell her I already do that
but I remembered all the ways
Mr. Borden had of embarrassing us
those first few days of school
and stopped myself from saying it
just in time

Joe raised his hand & asked, *Write about what?*
and I liked her answer, *Whatever's on your mind . . .*

A NEW MOM STORY

This Halloween some of the boys from my class
tipped over Grandpa's outhouse
Mom went after them
with a broom
screaming like a banshee
and they took off running
By then the damage was done
It took Joe & Gramps
all next day to right it
make it secure again

At supper Gramps told a story
about when he was young
how he helped some
bigger boys
on a dare
tip over Old Man Olson's
outhouse
with him in it
Whoooeee! Was he surprised
Sittin' there with the
Monkey Ward catalog and a
flashlight
one minute
and layin' down the next

We all had a good laugh
and Mom said, wiping
at her wet eyes
Well, Dad, at least you
weren't in
this one!

WISHING OURSELVES BACK TO

All this time I've been remembering my brother
blaming him for pulling Mom & Gram
& Daddy every which way from Sunday
I was forgetting how Tuck & I grew
for seven years side by side
how we slept in the same room
& ate the same food
& took baths in that old tin tub together

Today I saw Beth's brother, Bill
shove Pig Thomas in the chest
heard him say, *Leave my sister alone, Pig . . .*
and in a hot & terrible flash I remembered how
one time skinny & sickly as Tuck was
when that creepy Tommy Olson
pinched & twisted my nose
Tuck walked up to him
grabbed his ear & jerked

He jerked so hard
Tommy sat down right where he stood
Tuck put his arm around me, said
Leave my sister alone . . .

I didn't think much of it at the time
but now I see how all along
I've been blaming Tuck for dying
but he couldn't help it his heart was bad
and I guess mostly I wish
we could climb back into one of those days
before tornado season
a day when my dad was still working on the river
my mom filling the house with rich baking smells
Tuck & I at the table beside her coloring
& reading & playing all our quiet story games

Maybe that's what my mom tries to do
wish herself back even further
before us all
when she was Gramps's little girl

I wonder what Gram or Gramps
wish themselves back to.

WHAT LIDIA WISHES
HERSELF BACK TO

I think I know what Lidia
wishes herself back to
and I wish that, too
almost more than anything

but there's something else

I can't help but wish
I could know
if my letter made any difference
if that was how they found out
if that was why Mr. Borden left

And more than that
I keep wondering whether
if I'd managed to speak up that awful day
if it would have made a difference

If I'd marched in right then
to see Mr. Walter
would he have listened
to me saying the words out loud

Would it have made
a difference
Could my loud, singing, crying
righteous words have
stopped Mr. Borden
before he did the second
angry, violent
thing

The truth is
I'll never know the answer.

THIS IS ALSO THE TRUTH

Beth & I caught a ride out to the Y
with her brother, Bill, & his friends
who were on their way to Hackensack
& in the Ojibwe store there was Lidia
working behind the counter
her little baby in a bouncer in the
open doorway to the back

Still so beautiful, but older
She seemed older now than either
Beth or me

I watched her eyes change from surprise
to something hard, distrust or maybe
jealousy & then get playful
teasing like they were last year

Aaniin ezhi-ayaayan, she said
& I knew it was a test to see
if I remembered the words
she taught me, How are you?

Aaniin, niijikwe, I answered
Hello, my friend
surprised at how clear my voice
rang out in that quiet birch bark room
Ni mino-ayaa . . . I am fine

Beth, I said, filling up the quiet
that followed, *I want you to meet
my friend, my niijikwe
Lidia White Cloud . . .*

NOW I'VE SEEN THAT BABY

We oohed & aahed over him
gurgling & bouncing
pushing off with
the tips of his tiny toes

Lidia said his name was Melvin

Then we bought a bunch of beads
to make friendship bracelets
said, *See you again sometime*
and hiked the railroad tracks back to town

The truth is, now I've seen that baby
seeing how much he looks
like his father
the truth is, Lidia won't ever dare
come back to school again.

KEEP ON SETTING THE WORDS FREE

When my mother saw my report card
what Mrs. Olaffson said about my poems
she looked at me in a funny transparent way
like she was seeing through me
to some distant galaxy

All she said was, *Hmmmmmmm*

Then yesterday a big box came
in a delivery truck & inside was
a Smith Corona typewriter
a real little one, lightweight, easy to press
the keys

I didn't know how much I wanted
some kind of praise from
my mother until
that gift arrived

But wasn't it just like her
to reward me for something I've been doing
ever since I can remember
It's only just now she is able to see

But that's okay, it feels good just the same
so I opened my mouth
& said, *Thanks, Mom, it's beautiful*
& saw the light break
on her face like a summer day

And I think
maybe what this means is
she's waking up a little & maybe
during this long, hard time
we've taken
more than one little step
toward each other.

MY MOTHER IN A RIGHTEOUS RAGE

Today when I got home from school
my mom was crying on the couch
a bunch of papers in her hand
more of them
spread out around her
like she'd read them & dropped them
hot potatoes

It wasn't till I got close I saw
she was reading my hidden poems
ones I'd written about Lidia
ever since that first day
Lidia's words about her mother
shook me to my soul

I grabbed for them, started in to
tell her she had no business
looking at them
without my permission

Oh, honey, Mom said, *Why didn't you
tell me about it? Why didn't you tell me
what happened at school?*

And I realized she was crying
over what happened to Lidia
& I didn't know what to say

Why didn't you tell us? Mom asked
again. *I'd have gone straight to
the school board with this . . . if only
we'd known*

He's gone, I said, because I still
couldn't think
what else to say

That terrible, hateful, disgusting man!
she hollered, waving the papers
in her hand

And for the first time ever in my life
I was glad my mom was in a righteous rage.

THE LAST BIG BLIZZARD

Snow started falling late this afternoon
& now the wind is blowing it sideways
Thin & stinging, sharp particles
in the deceptive shape of snowflakes
it sticks to the highway
slicks into a sheet of black ice

March blizzard, Gramps says
shaking his head, takes his new tubes of paint
& heads for his easel
Gram's downstairs, her own kind of art
a chicken potpie, the smell telling me
supper will be a masterpiece
For once Mom's curled in a corner chair
reading a book. *Thank goodness I have*
tonight off, she says

The sounds my fingers make on this keyboard
late winter ice tapping at our windows
sharp *flick click* of Gram's after-supper solitaire
static on Gramps's radio, one ear listening for
cancellations, road closures, school closures
A gust of wind rattling windows in their sills

How about a piece of that blueberry pie, Lil?
Gramps says. Mom & Gram rise as one
& head for the basement kitchen
I'll start the coffee, Mom says, *You two
keep on with what you're doing . . .*

Gramps keeps right on painting
Out of the corner of my eye I can see
he's working on a summer scene tonight
looks like it might be Bear Island on a windy day
I can tell he's painting from memory
dabbing colors together
mixing until he's satisfied

I wonder if I could ever learn
to paint like he does
or play the piano like my mom
or bake pies like Gram

But right now my fingers rock
on my new keyboard
the sounds & rhythms of remembering
my story its own drumming
setting the words free.

IN A HURRY TO GET TO SUMMER

It's finally spring again here in Northern Minnesota
all rain & wind or soft clouds floating
in a baby blue sky
Some days there's thunder & lightning
and afterwards you can almost
watch the grass grow
leaves on the birch trees
unfurling into the sweetest green
like they're in as much hurry as we are
to get to summer

We don't have tornadoes here
waterspouts sometimes on the lake
every once in a while
a tornado warning
a ways south

And root cellars are just for vegetables.

ESCAPING TORNADO SEASON

I was remembering the other day
about my dad telling me
There's no escaping tornado season . . .

What I think is that sometimes
you can hunker down
to save yourself

like when we came up into the light
after that tornado
& surveyed the damage

So I'm thinking, maybe what matters
is how you get on with your life
after that, or maybe
it's who else you let yourself love

And I think Mom & I are like
Gram's willow tree

That old tree is so strong
it waves its branches
in every whirling summer wind

Maybe that's what happens
You put down roots right where you are

Then you can stand up & holler
at the next tornado about to
dip from biscuit clouds

Well, come on then if you must,
come on . . .

MEMORIAL DAY AGAIN

I got up early
so I could ride my bike
out to the cemetery
be alone out there, just my dad & me
& Tuck

I wanted to build my dad a grave house
but it's like so many other things
I can build only with words

So I used Lidia's beads to make him
a string with his initials on it
and I made one for Tuck, too

I slipped my brother's into a crack
in the holder where we put
the begonias each year
& said a prayer

Daddy's I hid in the soft dirt between
the grassy mound & his stone

And I said the words Lidia had written
all those long months ago
at first for my father & then
for all of us lost in tornado season

So you will know I'm thinking of you always
So you will know you're never alone

So you will know there will never be a time when
I will stop missing you . . .

ACKNOWLEDGMENTS

With special thanks to:
Linda Townsdin, best bud since the beginning; Christie Logan for her believing heart; our chosen family—Sam & Babs, Ben & Liz, JH, CL, Mr. Mike, Mesan; Marilyn Morton, partner in writing crimes and all the other members of the Society of Children's Book Writers and Illustrators who have been so supportive over the years (especially Judy Enderle, Stephanie Gordon, Sue Alexander, and the Cottage Poets—Anita, Bonnie, Jeanene, Keri, Marilyn, Mary Ann, & Patsy); José Luis Vargas and the entire Educational Opportunity Program "family." And the real families behind the stories—the Sarffs, Spantons, Sautbines, Nakagawas, and Williamses (with special thanks to Evelyn Williams). Deep appreciation to my remarkable editor, Rosemary Brosnan. Last, but never ever least—my beloved immediate family—husband, Gordon Nakagawa, and daughter, Jennifer Williams.

Additional thanks to:
Walker High School English teacher Chuck Beckman (my Mrs. Olaffson)—the first teacher to tell me I was a writer. Dennis Jones and Anna Bendickson, American Indian Studies Program at the University of Minnesota, for invaluable assistance with the Ojibwe language used in this book. Larry Aitken, spiritual advisor of the Leech Lake Reservation—for our conversations about Ojibwe culture then and now. The Minnesota Historical Society, Cass County Historical Society, Birchbark Books in Minneapolis for its wonderful selection of Ojibwe resources: *A Concise Dictionary of Minnesota Ojibwe* (edited by John D. Nicols and Early Nyholm, University of Minnesota Press, 1995); *Daga Anishinaabemoda* by Dennis and Lorraine Jones (a word list and phrase book of introductory Ojibwe); *Our Ojibwe Grammar*, vol. 1, by Rick Gresczyck (Gwayakogaabo), Eagle Works. I appreciate all the help given me—any mistakes are my own.